The Pandora Gambit

By

Levi Samuel

This book is dedicated to George Canfield.

You may be an asshole, but you're our asshole!
You're never one to sugar coat.
Because of that, we're all better off having you in our lives.
Even when I disagree with what you're saying,
I promise I'll always make a point to listen.

Thank you for purchasing this book. Your support is what allows me to do what I love.

The Pandora Gambit is unlike any other book I've written. I can't tell you how happy I am that so many people have enjoyed it.

When I started writing this story, I was a little concerned it wouldn't have the kind of following it deserves. It wasn't a story issue. That flows nicely considering the style I decided to go with. It was more a concern that this isn't your traditional urban fantasy. Vampires and werewolves have flooded the market for urban fantasy books. I didn't want this to be another casualty in that war. Moreover, I didn't want to contribute to what I feel is an already over populated niche. Instead, I wanted a low-fantasy, low-magic, epic set in modern day. I believe I achieved that. At the very least, if it didn't happen in this installment, it has plenty of room to grow.

Again, thank you for purchasing, and please leave a review. They help us more than you know.

Additionally, if you'd like exclusive access to a free book, please consider subscribing to my newsletter at, http://eepurl.com/dxRUvL

Contents

Chapter 1
Pandora's Box

A gentle breeze blew across the open top of the silver-flaked, red Maserati. It sat in an empty lot overlooking the bay. It'd been a long night and Ray Bradley hadn't gone home yet. He leaned against the polished hood, feeling the bright sunlight upon his face. Taking a bite of his burger, a static-buzz echoed from the driver's seat. Glancing over his shoulder, he anticipated what was to follow.

A distorted voice came through along with several loud pops. "Code-Thirty. Shots fired at Bayshore Drive and 91st Terrace. Officer down. Requesting immediate assistance!"

"All units converge on location!" A woman's voice replied.

"So much for lunch." Ray tossed his partially eaten burger into a trash bin that had been chained to an angled palm tree. Running his hands along his tan suit jacket, he ensured any crumbs that may have clung to him were dislodged. Opening the door, he tossed the radio into the passenger's seat and jumped in, firing up the engine.

Tires squealed as he shifted into reverse and backed out of the lot. Working the clutch, he found first gear and hit the gas. The car accelerated without flaw, climbing through the gears. Weaving between cars, Ray glanced at the speedometer. The red needle sat idle at seventy-two. She had plenty of pedal left, but there was no telling when one of these idiots would turn into him, and time was of the essence, meaning there was none for an accident. Cutting the wheel, he blew through a red light, missing a garbage truck by two car lengths. Plenty of time to get out of the way. Smiling his contempt, Ray melded into the car. She handled like a dream. And he would do everything he could to protect her. Technically speaking, it wasn't his. It was on loan, courtesy of the Miami Vice Police Department. Ray Bradley was a police sergeant in the narcotics division. And in Miami you had to look the part if you were going to play the game.

Seeing the light ahead, Ray hoped it would change before he reached it. Traffic was too heavy. He'd have to slow and wait if it didn't. To his fortune, it shifted from red to green just as he arrived. The car leaned hard, tilting against the suspension. Tires gripping, she slid around the corner of 72nd and onto Biscayne Boulevard without breaking traction. Again, he pressed the accelerator, passing cars left and right. In no time, he reached his turn onto 88th and stair stepped the last couple miles to 91st Terrace.

Flashing red and blue lights illuminated the distance. He was close enough now, he'd have to play it careful. He couldn't risk being seen by any of his contacts. At least not in an official capacity. He'd seen many TV shows make that mistake. Yet nobody ever recognized them. Real life didn't work that way. Of course, real criminals didn't want anything to do with the cops either. But that didn't mean they didn't watch what was happening just like everybody else. An undercover cop being seen at a crime scene was a death warrant on these streets. Everybody was connected. All it took was one scumbag to recognize you and the game would be over. That was the day you retire and hope you made it home. But most never made it that far.

Ray flew across 10th Avenue. The entire right side of the street was stacked with metal shipping containers. He knew the area well. Smugglers were notorious for hiding their product among import goods. The trick was getting a line on where and when. More often than not the goods hit the street, leaving them to clean up the mess after the fact. It made the job harder, but that was part of it. Nobody ever went undefeated in this line of work.

Whipping the car sideways, Ray slid onto an asphalt roadway between two stacks of containers. Following the road, he dodged a large forklift hauling what appeared to be a yacht that had been wrapped in thick, white plastic. Correcting, he continued on, drawing ever closer to the scene. Searching the gaps between containers, he pulled into an empty space and turned the engine off. He'd have a short walk before he could see what was happening, but at least his cover would remain intact.

Pushing the button on the key fob, the trunk popped open. Stripping his sports coat, Ray laid it over the trunk lid, seeing the Huntsman label on the inner liner. He was pleased they'd spared no expense on his image. If only there were a few more choices available. Ray unscrewed the spare tire cover and removed the false bottom. Careful to keep any grease or dirt from marring him. He stuck his hand into the compartment and secured his badge. It was dangerous keeping it with him, but in instances such as these, the good guys needed to know how to identify their own. Placing the chain necklaced badge around his neck, he gently laid his jacket with the loose cover and closed the trunk.

Machine gun fire drew his attention. Peeking between the metal containers, Ray could see the glow of police lights. An officer lay in the street beside his squad car. A pool of red formed beneath him. More gunshots echoed. Moving to a better vantage point, Ray searched for the shooter. It obviously wasn't the cops. They typically didn't use machine guns. Stepping to the edge, he glanced around the corner. There was a wide section that would allow him full view of the standoff. But that also meant he would be in full view of them. An idea came to mind. Reaching into his pocket, Ray pulled his smart phone. Turning on the camera, he swiped the screen, swapping to selfie mode. Pinching the image, it zoomed briefly. He stuck it past the threshold, angling so he could watch the screen. Ray studied the relayed image, hoping to see anything that would help him end this, and allow his brothers in blue the chance to go home to their families.

An old van, painted two-tone between light and dark brown, sat diagonally across the street, blocking both lanes. The rear doors were open and what appeared to be a blue plastic drum had fallen out. There were a couple bullet holes in the barrel and a syrup-thick liquid pooled on the blacktop. It appeared bright red. Too bright for blood. Angling the phone, Ray saw several more drums in the back of the van. "What's so important about those barrels that's worth dying for?" He asked himself. Movement caught his attention. On the far side of the van a masked face passed the front passenger window.

A man stepped from behind the open rear door and squeezed off several shots into the defensively positioned squad cars.

The police ducked behind their engines, hoping to avoid any stray bullets.

No sooner than the cops ducked, the man took cover behind the van and made his way back toward the front.

Ray knew he had only a moment. It was risky but if it ended the situation quicker, it was worth it. Tucking his phone away, he drew his pistol and took aim at the passenger window. The nickel-plated Colt felt good in his hand. The wood grips had been custom made for him. And the sights had been upgraded to fiber optics.

As expected, the man passed into view. Taking aim, Ray exhaled and squeezed the trigger. His target hit the ground. Ray watched him for a moment from beneath the van. He hadn't moved. Feeling he'd been in the open too long, Ray took cover behind the container and retrieved his phone. Positioning it so he could see the officers, he counted at least five dead, and another few injured. This area should have been swarming by now. Where the hell was everybody?

A few cops peeked over their hoods, noticing the lack of gunfire. Seeing the gunman laying in the street, they cautiously moved forward. Another burst of machine gun fire sent them running for cover. One of the officers was hit, unable to get to safety.

Ray watched from the safety of his phone. The second gunman didn't take any chances. No sooner than the officer hit the ground, another burst of bullets tore into his prone body, ensuring he wouldn't get up. This had to end. He tried to get a view of the gunner but couldn't see him. The angle of the bullets suggested he was ahead of the van and to the right. There was no way to get a clear shot from here. He'd have to move along the side of the container, or try to get a shot off between the stacks. The latter was going to be next to impossible considering the last pair he'd seen that weren't pressed tightly together was four stacks down. He'd narrowly been able to see the brick wall across the street through that one, let alone the action. Taking a deep breath, Ray ensured his badge was visible. It was a great risk he was taking, but he seemed to be the only one in position to take it. Tucking his phone away, Ray stepped out and cautiously walked along the dinged, red container, keeping his back as close to it as possible. He only hoped the cops didn't shoot him on sight. Such would be his luck.

Reaching the far end, Ray spun, surveying the scene from behind his firearm. He recalled where he believed the shooter to be. He just had to find him before they found him. From here, Ray noticed the van had crashed into another car. A white Volkswagen Golf it appeared. Steam rose from the hood, and the side of the van was marred in places and scuffed white. The angle of the VW was off. There was no way it was a side collision. The van had run straight into it, creating a T-bone scenario. Ray could now see where the white paint came from. A squad car sat to his left, mangled around a tree. Those were the lights he'd seen during his approached. Evidence suggested the van was fleeing pursuit. When the squad car got beside it, the driver turned into it, trying to bump it off the road. When that didn't work, they opened fire. He could see the bullet holes in the passenger side of the mangled cop car. There was a good chance the driver was hit and killed before his car ran into the tree. Inadvertently, it was the Volkswagen that had stopped the van.

The clicks of a freshly loaded firearm echoed from across the street. Ray knew what was coming next. He was either going to be in perfect position to end this, or he would be the first to die in this volley of bullets. It would all depend on his speed and accuracy.

The gunman stepped from between two buildings, gun in front of him, its aim tied to his stance. Turning on foot, he positioned to fire upon the cops. He had to keep them distracted long enough for backup to arrive. That was the only way they were going to get the shipment out of here before the humans had a chance to discover what it was. It was best they didn't know. From the corner of his eye, he saw a man across the street, aimed and ready to fire. He wore a blue, button-up shirt, and tan suit pants. The sleeves were rolled about the elbows. His appearance didn't say cop, but the badge hanging around his neck sure did. It was too late. He hadn't counted on him being there, having picked up where his dead companion left off. It was strange. He didn't even know the dead man's name. That wasn't part of the job. It didn't matter. He'd made a mistake. And for that his kind was going to have troubling days ahead.

Ray saw his chance. His heart raced within his chest. The gunman had looked right at him from beneath the black ski mask. All he had to do was pull the trigger and he'd be no more. But he hadn't. The gunman had passed him over and taken aim on the cops. It was now or never. He couldn't risk giving the man another chance. And a wounding shot wouldn't disable the threat, let alone protect his cover. Ray felt his firearm kick, ejecting the spent casing. He could almost watch the bullet fly across the street toward its target. It struck with perfect precision. The gunman collapsed where he stood, dropping his weapon.

Ray scanned the area. He needed to be certain the threat was eliminated, but he couldn't rightly walk out in the open. There were bound to be witnesses all over the place. Last thing he needed was to be recognized. Retrieving his phone, he dialed from memory. He couldn't risk saving the number into the device. Such a mistake could cost his life. Money was the voice of this city. And money could buy nearly everything. Phone records, testimonies, illegal firearms. You name it, there was always someone to sell it. Instead, they'd gone a simpler route. Google was one of many companies that had a phone forwarding feature. You could set up a new number that was forwarded to your personal or business line. It was a cheap and easy way of having a second, unlisted, and unidentified number, without having to go through the hassle of setting it up with the phone company. Additionally, since the signal bounced, hackers had a slightly more difficult time of locking the ownership down.

"Anderson." An aged voice answered on the other end.

"Captain, Ray Bradley here. I responded to this 245-B, officer down. I've eliminated two suspects. I believe the situation is contained but I cannot verify."

"Understood Sergeant. What's the 11-40?"

"Multiple dead, multiple wounded. I'd advise locking down the area and doing a full sweep during cleanup. We also need to get forensics down here. The suspects were hauling barrels of something. At least one barrel is leaking onto the street."

"10-4, Sergeant. The officers on site can handle it from here. Go home and get some rest. I'll collect your official report from the night drop."

"Understood, Captain."

The station house had a steady flow of traffic. A digital clock hung from the wall over the Captain's door. It currently read 11:21 in bright red numbers. A plastic palm tree sat beside the window, swaying gently in the light breeze airing out the building. A row of three connected chairs sat on the other side, occupied by a single man dressed in baggy street clothes and a blue baseball cap.

"Bradley, get in here!" Captain Anderson called from his office.

Ray pulled himself from the plastic seat. He adjusted his hat in an attempt to protect his identity. It didn't do much, but obscurity was all he could hope for. He already missed the feel of the silk shirts and expensive suits. It was a life style he'd never expected to find himself in. Yet the last three months had shown him a world previously unknown. Before that he was a simple kid, a few years out of the academy. His time in the army had taught him the majority of the tactical skills, but it left something to be desired with normal human interaction. He didn't much care for people. And being a cop didn't help matters. Spending day in and day out surrounded by the scum of the earth kept him looking over his shoulder. Everybody was a suspect until proven otherwise. It made having a private life extremely difficult. At least when he wasn't working. While on the job, he had little difficulty. It was an acting game. He'd found it difficult to play the role at first. But it got easier. After a while the lines blurred and being morally indifferent became a tool to stay alive. Playing a criminal was different than actually being one. Sure, he had to break a few laws here and there. But they were sanctioned by the department. Beforehand or after made little difference, though before was preferred. There wasn't always time to get approval before the proverbial shit hit the fan. Criminals were often sporadic, heat of the moment types. They may have had a plan in motion, but they were known to change it at the last minute in an attempt to root out any leaks that may have developed in their systems. It kept the cops off their backs and let them know if they had a traitor in their ranks. If a warehouse got raided when the shipment was scheduled to be picked up, but the cops arrived to an empty location because the product had already been moved, there was bound to be some paranoia. Like everything else, it was a tool.

Stepping into the medium sized office, Ray noticed a large man sitting against the wall. He was gruff looking. Strong jaw line, thick arms threatening to tear out the stitched seams of his sleeves. Knowing nothing about the man's intelligence, his appearance led to a single term. Brute, was the first to come to mind. Ray closed the wood and glass door and turned to face his captain, refusing to take a seat. "Yes, Sir?"

"I got the lab results back from that shoot out the other day. The liquid found in those barrels had high levels of something that resembles a mix between cocaine and opium, but neither narcotic could be found. In fact, the samples were void of any known narcotic. I think we may be looking at a new chemical compound. I sent the report to the DEA, CDC, and the Bureau of Narcotics. Which brings me to my next point."

The man sitting against the wall stood and straightened his suit jacket. The wool had been stretched, creating a patchy mixture of light and dark gray threads. He cupped one meaty hand over the other and rested them together in front of his waist.

"Sergeant, meet Special Agent William Crumble from the DEA. Apparently, this new drug hit the streets of Chicago pretty hard. They're calling it Pandora. Agent Crumble is here to keep the same thing from happening to our city."

Ray turned to face the large man. He seemed even bigger now that he was standing. "Nice to meet you, Agent. It'll be good to have some outside assistance for a change." Ray shook his hand, dwarfed by comparison.

"Actually, Sergeant, this is his investigation. And since you're already in position to get a lead on where it's coming from, you get to help him."

"What?" Ray glanced from the brute to Captain Anderson, and back again. "Captain, you can't expect me to play babysitter for this guy. Look at him. He could pass for hired muscle, sure. But nobody's gonna make a deal with a bodyguard. He's a nobody. People don't talk to nobodies."

"This isn't a request, Sergeant. This case just became your top priority. Do whatever it takes to keep this crap off our streets!"

Chapter 2
Brothers in Arms

A light layer of frost had settled on the ground. The late-autumn air was cold but not freezing. Rattling tin could be heard in the steady breeze, wrapping its way around any lip, edge, or opening it could find. A long runway rested between several large hanger warehouses. Lights beamed into the sky from either side, doing little more than marking the sides. Across from the only warehouse that remained lit, despite the decommissioning of the site six months prior, a unit of soldiers waited in the shadows. They were spread out, two to four men per team. Nearly twenty in total, each holding position, watched the surrounding entrances while awaiting orders.

"Team Two. I've got eyes on target."

"Copy that, Team Two. Stand fast. Go on my mark."

A blue glow hit the side of the surrounded building, spotlighting the rusted tin siding comprising the outer wall. The lights trailed the entire side of the building and turned, revealing the LED headlights on a stretched Lincoln Navigator. The glossy black paint reflected the street lamps outside the yard. Turning in front of the hanger, the large bay door on the front-center wall slowly raised, illuminating the gravel roadway outside. A small white and blue jet showed through the partially open door, resting idle on the far side of the largely empty warehouse. Several men dressed in suits, stood guard inside the door. A collection of others waited near a folding table not far from the jet. The Navigator turned and pulled into the building, the door closing as soon as it was clear.

"That's our cue. Team Four, move when ready. Eliminate any resistance you encounter."

Crum squeezed the pistol grip of his MP5. The sling was wrapped tight around his left bicep, holding the weapon at the ready. He wore black tactical clothing and his chest was enwrapped in heavy body armor. He watched the steam roll from his breath in the cool night air. There was no doubt his fingers would be numb if not for the reinforced gloves protecting them. This was a raid. And while he'd undergone them before, he was still nervous. In a few moments hell was going to break loose, and he'd be at ground zero.

"You ready, partner?"

Crum made eye contact. Wright was nearly as tall as him, but had substantially less muscle. It wasn't his fault really. Elves were naturally less stocky. They also weren't known for being friendly toward orcs. But that didn't stop their partnership from becoming more than a working relationship. Crum nodded. "Let's do this."

Wright pressed the com button mounted to his armor. "Team Four, going in." He and Crum darted across the alleyway, moving into position beside the wall the limo had bright-lighted moments earlier. He gave the signal, watching another team step from shadow and disappear around the corner.

Ensuring Wright was on point, Crum released his weapon, letting the sling catch it. Removing one of his gloves, he ran his bare hand along the tin siding. It was easy enough to see the interior runners. All you had to do was follow the row of screw-heads. Finding the wall supports themselves would prove somewhat more difficult. But the cold would help with that. The heat inside the warehouse would warm the metal where there was no brace. Now all he had to do was find the cold spots and avoid them. Quickly mapping out his entry point, Crum pulled a roll of thick tape from his pocket and pressed it against the siding. He marked a large rectangle, ensuring the corners overlapped. Leaving a few inches on the bottom points, he removed a small detonator from his pocket and pulled the pre-cut insulation to expose bare wire. Attaching one wire to each tail, he took a few steps back, replaced his glove, and gripped his weapon. Nodding to Wright, he readied to push the button.

Returning his focus to the shadows, Wright activated his com once again. "Team Four, ready and waiting."

"Team Six, ready and waiting."

"Team Three, ready and waiting."

Each team sounded off. After a moment of silence, the ear bud transmitted again.

"All teams enter on three— two— one."

A snap echoed from inside the box and the tape exploded, melting the metal in an instant. Wasting no time, Crum dropped the spent detonator and slammed his shoulder into the loose siding. It fell inward. He rushed through the entry point, chucking a cylinder across the room.

Several metal canisters skated along the smooth concrete floor. White smoke billowed from each one, obscuring vision. Several rapid pops echoed all around, their location signaled only by muzzle flash.

Seeing one of the suited figures to the left, not fully enveloped in smoke, Crum took aim and squeezed the trigger. His weapon fired in rapid succession, vibrating in his hand. The figure hit the ground. A roar echoed to his right. It only took a minute to realize someone had started the jet. The smoke began to fade, rapidly being pulled through the massive engines mounted behind each of the side wings. "Wright, the plane!" Crum signaled and charged toward it. He didn't know how it was going to get out. The hanger doors were closed. But someone started the engine. They had to have some escape plan, even if their only option was to bust through. For all he knew they had a remote opener in the cockpit. Bullets whizzed by, narrowly missing him.

Three armed suits stood at the bottom of the steps leading to the sealed door on the side of the jet. Each was aimed and ready to kill.

Pointing his own weapon, Crum fired. One dropped. He took aim at a second and squeezed the trigger. A single round expelled, and his weapon clicked empty, refusing to cock. That was it. He'd forgotten to track his ammunition. Now he was staring down two low-born elves, no stronger than fifth generation, and he was out of ammo. It was a hell of a way to go, but it was his mistake. Closing his eyes, expecting the worst, two pops echoed behind him and the suits dropped. Crum glanced over his shoulder to find Wright standing behind him. He hadn't yet lowered his weapon. "Thanks, brother."

Wright nodded and darted to the left, disappearing into the fading smoke.

Squeezing the lever behind the magazine, Crum pulled it free and stuffed it in his cargo pocket. Locking the action back, he slammed another mag into place and released the bolt to reload his weapon. Moving toward the jet, the engines began to balance out, signifying it was ready to move. He had to hurry. If they got away there was no telling where they'd turn up next. Glancing toward the Navigator, the lights were still on and the doors were open. Whoever was in it had already made their move, likely aboard the plane. Only now did he realized just how much of the smoke had been dispersed. Little more than a light haze remained in the air. But that would work to his advantage. Most of the suits had fallen, leaving a few near the door and however many were in the jet. But he had to keep it from leaving. Crum glanced to the ceiling above the hanger door. Two large motors hung from steel frames. A drive rod extended out the sides, adjoining both. Twin sprockets were secured beside each door track. And a thick chain ran from the sprockets to a smaller one near the top of the door. Perhaps if he could disable the motors, he could trap the jet. Taking aim, Crum fired. Bullets tore through the case and sparks danced around the frame. They disappeared long before hitting the ground. Doing the same to the second motor, he returned his attention to the jet. It was beginning to roll. He had to act fast. Shooting it was out of the question. He couldn't risk an explosion. That would vaporize the drug and was likely to infect upwards of twelve city-blocks, depending on how far the wind carried it. Crum searched for anything he could use. The warehouse was nearly empty. Whatever they'd stored here had clearly already been loaded on the plane, likely the drug. Only a few wooden pallets remained against the side wall. Those wouldn't do him much good, unless— He had an idea. Inspecting the folding table, he was pleased to see it wasn't one of the flimsy plastic ones. This one had some girth. It had a thick wooden top, and the frame and legs were metal. If that wouldn't do the trick, he didn't know what would. Dropping his weapon, caught by the nylon strap attached to him, Crum lifted the table overhead and carried it toward the left side turbine. He'd thought about throwing the table into the blades. But there was no guarantee he'd be able to throw it straight, even if it would fit. There was also no guarantee the blades wouldn't just kick it back out. It could hit him and that wouldn't help anyone. There was also the matter of blowing it up, which could result in the aforementioned problem. Instead, it was commonly known that turbine engines required large amounts of air to function. That meant all he had to do was restrict the air flow. Heaving the table, Crum slammed the flat top over the air intake and held fast, hoping it would do the trick.

It took little more than the gesture for the engine to suck the table tight against it, covering the intake completely. The turbine began to growl from lack of air.

Crum could feel the building heat. He needed to get clear. If the engine were to come apart, he didn't want to be anywhere near it. But at least the plane itself should remain intact. As if the thought triggered something, black smoke billowed from the clogged engine and the turbine slowed to a stop, halting the plane. A bright flame shot from the back side and the engine died, winding down with a grinding roar. The table hit the ground and fell to its side. Now was his chance. He needed to gain access before they restarted the engines and made a run for it.

Charging up the stairs, Crum grabbed the stainless-steel door latch. It was recessed to aid aerodynamics which made it difficult to get a good hold. Straining against it, the lock flexed beneath his strength. If he could get just a little more leverage, there was no doubt the lock would break and he'd have entry. All of this would be over if he could just get inside. The four years of investigations, undercover assignments, stakeouts, interrogations, and ground work that had led to this moment would finally be at an end. The bad guys would finally pay for their crimes. But he had to get to them first.

A final volley of gun shots echoed through the warehouse. Had Crum not been so distracted, perhaps he would have noticed. Pulling as hard as he could, Crum's muscles bulged beneath his black, tactical shirt. Sweat clung to his brow. But it paid off. He felt the pop and the handle rotated. Pulling the door open, the inside walkway was lined in small lights, as if he needed a guide to know which way to go. He didn't know what awaited him inside the windowless jet, but it was likely they were armed. Crum readied his weapon and stepped inside.

The interior was unlike any plane he'd ever seen, much less been in. Commercial airliners were crowded and uncomfortable. And those small seats left you feeling like you were sitting on someone's lap. His size didn't help in that regard. This however, was anything but uncomfortable. It may as well have been a small nightclub. A fully stocked bar and kitchen ran the length of the main cabin. A polished, silver pole ran to the ceiling from the center of a small stage to the side. There were a number of plush chairs scattered about the chamber, positioned for comfort more than anything. And at the rear, a closed door separated him from his mission.

"Crum'Bul, what's your position?" Wright's voice echoed through the earbud.

Pressing the PTT button, Crum replied. "Nearing objective completion. The Warlords are barricaded in the back of the jet." He didn't much care for the code name his targets had been given. It empowered them further, which he believed was a mistake. But it was better than using their given names. They were traitors to their kind, using humans to further their archaic quest of world domination. While there was plenty of room for improvement between human-supe relations, another name he didn't much care for, using them like cattle to further their goals was against the code. And without the code there was nothing to keep the humans from wiping the rest of them out.

Crum approached the door and took a step to the side. Rapping his thick fist against the sealed barrier, several shots tore through the material. Timing it out, he slammed his open palm against the wall, and raked downward. Stomping once, the entire plane shook. It wasn't much, but perhaps to a trapped animal it would sound as if he'd been hit and fallen.

As he'd hoped, footsteps approached. The silver handle rattled, and the door slowly opened.

A smile came to his face, stretching thin lips around his lengthened tusks. Crum slammed his shoulder into the opening door, hitting the figure on the other side. The resin cracked beneath the force, and the bottom hinge broke free. Wasting no time, Crum ripped the door open and grabbed the stunned figure.

It was one of the warlords, an elf, third generation from the smell of him. Wrapping his meaty hand around the weapon's slide, he tore it from the elf's grip, and slammed him against the wall. The fiberglass broke and the elf fell limp.

Three remained. Lifting his victim, Crum pulled the broken door open and stepped inside, using the unconscious warlord as a shield. "Lower your weapons and surrender. We have orders to kill, and you're surrounded!"

A gunshot echoed in his ears. It wasn't his own. He knew that much. And it wasn't from any of the warlords. They looked just as confused as he did. Pain erupted in his chest. Crum glanced at the small hole in the left side of his body armor. How was that possible? It was reinforced to withstand gunshots. Even armor-piercing bullets were next to useless outside of twenty yards. But at point-blank range? The armor wasn't designed to absorb such. It needed time to slow the bullet and disperse the impact. Looking over his shoulder, Crum saw a familiar face. "Wright?"

"I'm sorry, buddy. But I can't have you delaying my men any longer than you already have."

"But— why?" Crum's knees went weak. He stumbled and fell. He was growing dizzy. He wouldn't be able to fight it much longer.

"It's simple. We've lived in the shadows of humanity for too long. We're stronger, older, and far superior. Why do we have to hide who we are? It should be them bowing to us!" A rage was present in his voice. An anger Crum had never seen before. "I put this whole thing together. Even joined the WMD to impact both sides. But that ends now. We have everything we need to go global. I hope you'll understand that I can't bring you along. I know you too well. You'd try to stop me."

Crum heard the engines fire up again. Everything felt as if it was moving slow. He was getting tired. He wanted to speak. Wanted to say anything, but his voice wouldn't comply. He was paralyzed. But it fueled him. He was growing angry. He wanted to rip this plane apart with his bare hands, if only they'd respond.

Gesturing, Wright extended his thumb toward the door. "Toss both him and Loren out. No since in carrying dead weight. We're already loaded to capacity."

Two of the warlords marched forward, an orc and an elf. They strained against Crum's bulky frame but managed to lift him. Most of the weight found the orc's shoulder. Dragging him to the outside door, they threw him out.

Crum hit the small staircase and rolled to the ground. He landed on his side, facing the smaller front door. Barely able to hold his eyes open, he saw the rest of his unit. They laid dead around the Navigator. Why had he not stayed with them? Would any of this have happened if he hadn't taken matters into his own hands? It angered him. But he was helpless to do anything about it. Something hit his back, rolling him to his stomach.

The roar of the engines grew, along with the grinding of the burnt turbine, and the wheels started to move.

Crum saw the two warlords that had thrown him out. They stepped over his prone form, and rushed toward the sealed hanger doors. They were getting away. He'd failed. The past four years of his life were all a waste. And he let it all happen under his nose. A comfortable numb overcame him. He no longer hurt. But he had to sleep. Closing his eyes, the noise faded away and silence took him.

Blinding light burned into the darkness. Taking a deep breath, Crum's eyes shot open. He tried to get up, tried to fight, but found himself unable to move. He was strapped to a bed. An annoying beeping sound echoed somewhere out of sight. "Where am I?" While the words were in question, his tone made them a demand.

"Relax, Crum'Bul." The voice sounded familiar, but he couldn't place who it belonged to.

"When you failed to report, we went looking. I'm sorry to tell you, but your entire unit is gone. You were the only survivor. It turns out being dosed by Pandora is what saved your life." A grizzled orc stepped into view.

Crum recognized him immediately. "Director Kel'Gos?" His memory was fuzzy. Pieces flashed into mind, filling the blanks. He needed to say the orc's name to ensure his body was working again.

"What is it, son?" There was a genuine concern on the old orc's face.

"It's Wright, Sir. He betrayed us. He was running the warlords the entire time. Said he had everything he needed to go global."

"I feared we had a mole. Never suspected it was him. But too many things went wrong to not have someone on the inside sabotaging our progress."

"If you'll allow me, Sir. I'd like to take a team to track him down. Wright has to pay for what he's done."

"I don't disagree with you, soldier. But you're in no condition to go after him right now. And until we find some trustworthy recruits, I'm afraid this betrayal has set us back substantially. We lost two-thirds of our ground men in that raid. And two other units were ambushed at check-in last week. But we'll get him. And I'll make damn sure you have the support you need when we do. But for now, I need you to heal up. That bullet you were shot with was laced. The main effects have left your system but we need to be certain there's no lingering symptoms."

"What do you mean that's what saved my life?"

"I'm sure you felt the rage burning inside you. That's what Pandora does to our kind. Even while grievously wounded, it'll push you beyond your limits. But it's synthetic. When you come down, it hits hard. Your heart slowed to a near stop. Had that not happened, you would have bled out long before we found you. So, while the bullet should have killed you, the fact that it was laced is what saved your life. Anyway, rest up. I'll debrief you once you've been cleared for service."

The Pandora Gambit

Levi Samuel

Chapter 3
New Territory

The walls, ceiling, and floor were washed white, emitting a brilliant glow despite the lack of obvious light sources. Equally bland doors with a small, reinforced glass window lined the hall. There were no signs or identification markers of any kind. The door windows were the only evidence to what awaited upon the other side.

Crum walked along the narrow corridor, listening to his footsteps. Occasionally, he glanced through a window, seeing lab technicians hard at work through one. Another appeared to be a firing range. Though no sound escaped the room. The targets at the far end appeared to be alive. Holograms or executions, he couldn't be sure. It didn't really matter. The complex had hundreds of rooms and he hadn't been to more than twenty of them in the near ninety-five years he'd served. Truth was, he didn't care what secrets the WMD held. Though he had no delusions they were numerous. The only thing that mattered was the mission. Peaceful existence between humans and everything else. But that mentality may have been what led to Wright's betrayal. Not to mention the drug. If he'd taken more of an active interest in what was happening behind the scenes maybe he would have seen the signs before things got so bad. Maybe he could have saved his friend. But such thoughts wouldn't change what happened. It had happened. And it was his job to fix it.

How Wright had even learned about the drug was a different question all together. It was originally created during the first World War. And it appeared again during the second, when it had briefly gotten out in southern Germany and parts of France. The Germans attempted to weaponize it, nearly succeeding. But after a year-long investigation, that eventually led to the procurement of both the drug and its creator, an orc name Bur'Ell, both were locked away at an undisclosed location.

Bur'Ell was a renowned engineer and chemist when such terms were still fairly new. He and his wife resided in a small town outside London where they designed and built the electric tramway in 1902. But in late-spring, 1915, a German bomb hit Yarmouth, and Bur'Ell's wife was killed in the explosion. Soon after, he went to work creating a stimulant to make orc-kind stronger. His intention was to create a living weapon. A single unit of enhanced orcs would be able to decimate an entire army without need for food or rest. If it worked, it would level the playing field against both elves and humans. And considering orc reproduction had all but dwindled some five-hundred years prior, enhancing their natural abilities would have proved invaluable. But such hope was short lived. The drug, while increasing natural strength and heartiness in orcs, also induced an unquenchable rage that left the user drained once it'd run its course. Such exhaustion resulted in the death of many orcs, making its use ill-advised by orc hierarchy.

It was the secondary effects that promoted circulation and made it difficult to track. Bur'Ell started experimenting on anyone he could find. He soon discovered it had various effects on each of the races. A batch was stolen and reverse engineered, allowing the formula to leak into the world. A sect of elves took interest and began distributing it to further their own agenda.

Elven-kind was the first to integrate into human culture. They used the last of the wellspring, the only known source of magical power, to blanket the world in an illusion. It made humans unable to see things for what they truly were. This allowed them to exist together in peace, keeping the humans ignorant of their existence and thereby unable to take up arms as they had so long ago. That wasn't to say all humans were unaware of their shared world. Simply that the vast majority were kept in the dark to protect both sides.

But the drug changed all of that. The elves learned to manipulate the humans. Pandora opened the door, allowing any human under its influence to peer through the veil. That presented a threat to the balance. If the wrong human ever discovered their existence it could mean all-out war. And neither side would walk away unscathed. But that was just the beginning. Since the integration many elves had taken to mating with humans. And while the elven blood overpowered the human side as far as feature, each time it diluted further. Only a handful of purebloods remained, and they preferred to remain hidden.

While the wellspring was gone, the purebloods retained their innate magics, rumored to be a magical race at their core. The more diluted the blood, the less those abilities remained. By the third generation all magical ability was gone. But that didn't stop the elves from experimenting. The drug, mystical as it seemed, gave them a synthetic boost. A third generation registered as a second. A sixth gen felt like a third. And so on. Fortunately, it didn't last. Their bodies began building resistances near instantaneous. Which meant each time they used, it took more to do less. With their magics all but gone, they resorted to simpler tactics. Humans were extremely susceptible to suggestion. But the illusion that kept the elves, as well as all others hidden from their perception also blocked their influence. The elves found a loophole. Humans that used the drug were able to see them for what they were. And that meant they were susceptible once again. For that reason, they began calling the drug, Pandora.

In 1919, Pandora was being distributed through a number of alcohol suppliers. All it took was a single drop per bottle. Any human that partook involuntarily became part of a much larger plan. Crime rates spiked. Organized crime grew to record highs.

And the elves were behind it all. In a strategic attack, agents were placed within the human government. They did the only thing they could to get the drug off the streets. They made the delivery system illegal. Thirteen long years, they tracked the distributors, unable to find the head of the snake. They'd raid one supplier and two more would grow in its wake. But finally, in 1933, they ended it. The elves responsible for distribution were captured and Pandora disappeared for a time.

Reaching the end of the hall, Crum turned right, into another, identical corridor. Approaching the third door on the left, he twisted the knob and stepped through.

The large room held the same colorless tone as the rest of the compound. There were no windows or lights, yet it glowed a brilliant white that was nearly overbearing. Had it not been for the multiple gray cubicle walls, wooden desks, assortment of office chairs, and multi-colored computer screens resting upon each desk, it certainly would have been. A dull roar lingered in the air, along with a multitude of tapping keyboards. This was where information was gathered. Nothing happened anywhere without someone in this room being among the firsts to learn about it.

Hugging the sidewall, Crum made his way around the islands of cubicles and toward the large, glass walled office at the far end. Approaching the metal framed door, he saw the old orc within nod and hold up a finger.

Director Kel'Gos finished his phone call. Laying the receiver to rest on its base, he glanced at the agent standing outside his door. Waving him in, Kel'Gos pressed the button under his thick, oaken desk, unlocking the door.

"You wanted to see me, Director?"

"Take a seat, Crum'Bul." Kel'Gos awaited compliance before he continued.

Pulling the padded, fabric covered chair to the center of the room, Crum plopped down. He was glad the director understood the need for oversized chairs. Orcs were broader than most and the small chairs such offices usually offered were a tight fit.

"We may have found Wright."

"Where, Sir? I'll head that way immediately."

"I know you will, son. That's why I'm telling you about it. But we're gonna have to play this one a bit different than usual. As you know, we haven't had much luck finding new recruits. Seems Wright's made enough of a name for himself that nobody wants to risk finding themselves in his crosshairs. That means we're gonna have to rely on some outside assistance."

"I understand, Sir. What do you need me to do?"

Kel'Gos grabbed a cherry-stained wooden box from the edge of his desk. The corner caps and hinges were plated gold. Flipping the matching latch, he opened it and removed a thick cigar from inside. Closing the lid, he punched out the back side and primed it. Puffing briefly, Kel'Gos twisted the cigar in the torch flame, and blew a heavy cloud of smoke into the ventilation port overhead. "We intercepted a call this morning from Miami PD. Seems over three-hundred gallons of Pandora turned up in the back of a van after a shootout. The suspects were killed. I had their autopsy reports pulled so our guys could look at em. As suspected, they were elf-kind. I did some digging in the usual channels. Everything suggest Wright is in Miami." Grabbing a file folder from the stack in front of him, Kel'Gos handed it to Crum.

Several papers filled the folder. Printed photographs had wide-angle shots of Wright standing on a yacht. Some had him getting into or out of a car, Crum couldn't tell exactly which was the case from lack of movement. A map was dotted along the coast. Each blip appeared to be a heavy industrial section. The legend suggested they were suspected deposit sites. And an entire other folder rested inside, labeled Ray Bradley. Miami's lead on the case was a young human, late twenties. Though his latest psych-evaluation suggested he was in denial about his growing age. He'd been a cop for six years, spent the last three at a desk, before being promoted to detective-sergeant in the undercover narcotics investigations division. He'd had that role for a little over three months. Prior to his joining the police academy, he spent five years in the Army as a combat engineer where he'd done two tours overseas, before being honorably discharged after his convoy hit an IED. He spent two months in a coma. Flipping through the folders, Crum saw a one-way, first-class plane ticket.

"Your name will be William Crumble. You're the specialized DEA agent assigned to handle this case. While you'll be working with this human, this Ray Bradley, I've made it very clear that you're in charge. He is to assist you, not the other way around. Anything you need, if Miami can't get it, let me know."

"Yes, Sir!" Crum stood and started toward the door.

"Be careful, Crum'Bul. Wright may have been a friend once. But he's not anymore. Don't give him the chance to finish what he started on that jet."

Crum nodded and left. He needed to pack up. Miami was going to be a whole new world.

"Looks like we're gonna be working together." Crum extended his hand to the aggravated human. He couldn't blame him. This wasn't his ideal situation either. But there was more at stake than personal feelings. In a perfect world crime would be non-existent and neither of them would be needed. But the world was far from perfect. Liars lie, thieves steal, murderers kill, and traitors betray. There was nothing anyone could do to keep it from happening. But when it did happen, it was their responsibility to catch them and keep it from happening again.

Ray exhaled sharply. He didn't like it. How was he supposed to do his job with this guy on his heels? But the captain had been clear. He had no choice. Taking the meaty hand, he squeezed just hard enough to send the message. He'd obey orders. But he wasn't going to take it laying down. "Come on, Crumble. Let's see what we can do to get you a backstory."

They approached the elevator at the far end of the building. The doors opened as they approached, two street cops stepping out.

Ray entered and pressed the button for the first floor.

Crum stepped through as the stainless-steel doors began to close, sandwiching him briefly before they opened again. He entered completely and leaned against the corner furthest from the selection panel. The elevator wasn't overly large and he was afraid he was crowding Ray. "So, you work undercover?"

"Yeah."

The silence was unbearable. Some noise, any noise would have helped. Even the annoying elevator music that always plagued such places was absent, leaving them to stare at their own reflections until the doors allowed escape.

Ray rushed through the gap, turning the corner. If the upstairs offices were loud and crowded, this floor was a circus. Large fans blew near the open windows in a vain attempt to circulate what little air entered. Cops worked the phones and chatted among each other. Perpetrators waiting to be booked, but not high priority enough to already be in lock up, sat idle near their arresting officers. This was the bulwark and it was a mad house.

Approaching a gorgeous, brunette woman at one of the side desk, Ray leaned over, stealing a quick glance down the crevice of her slightly too-tight, red button-up shirt.

"I hope you got a good look. That's all you're ever gonna see."

"Hello to you too, Katelynn. You're looking exceptionally nice today."

"What do you want, Ray? I've got a murder-suicide down on Belle Meade. And a hit and run on 84th."

Crum made his way through the crowd. Most of them moved out of his way as soon as they saw his size. Approaching Ray, he awaited the human. They needed to get a lead on where Pandora was being imported. If they could find a dealer, that would lead to the distributor. And from there it was a short chain until they found Wright. But this wasn't his city. He didn't know where to look for a dealer. That was Ray's department. And apparently, he thought getting him a background was worthy use of their time. So, he'd humor it for a while.

"Who's your friend?" Katelynn trailed the behemoth from head to toe. He was easily six-foot-tall and had to weigh at least three-hundred pounds of pure muscle.

"Katelynn, this is Agent Crumble, DEA. Crumble, this is Katelynn Slack, homicide. We're working a case together. Need to get him a background before we hit the streets. I was hoping you'd put me in touch with your guy."

She shook his hand, returning her attention to Ray. "Yeah. He'll take some convincing though."

"What kind of convincing?" Ray pulled a wad of hundreds from his pocket. It didn't have the same effect as when he pulled it from his suit jacket.

"Couple hundred will get you an audience. But right now, he's in a collecting mood. Sometimes he wants a favor. Other times he wants a rare bottle of whiskey. Hell, once he asked me for a specific Power Ranger action figure."

"Not that it matters, but which one?"

"Hell, I don't know. It was blue and cost way more than it was worth." Katelynn grabbed a yellow Post It from her desk and wrote a number. "Give him a call. Worst he'll say is no."

"Thank you, doll."

"Yeah." Snatching her badge and pistol from the top right desk drawer, Katelynn clipped both onto her waist and squeezed past Ray, intentionally rubbing against him.

Watching her hips sway as she made for the stairs to the exit, Ray broke his gaze, realizing Crumble was staring at him. "Long story. We used to date."

"Your business. What do we do now?" Crum was growing impatient. There were things to do and Ray seemed more interested in chasing tail and wasting time than anything else.

"I need to get in touch with this guy. They call him the Score Keeper. When it comes to backstories, no one's better. His whole life is centered around collecting information. Anyone goes in the pen, he notes it. Someone dies, he keeps track. When you need an identity, he creates one tailored to you. Facts of your life will match with facts of your cover, keeping you from having to remember a bunch of lies. To my knowledge he's never had a blown cover due to the identity side of things."

"Do what you've got to do. Let's just get the ball rolling. I don't want to spend any more time here than I have to."

"Give me a couple hours to get in touch and see what he's charging. There's a coffee shop two blocks south on the right. I'll pick you up there around 5:00. Everything should be in order by then." Refusing to wait for objection, Ray turned and rushed toward the side door.

Making his way through the alley behind the police station, Ray stepped onto the side walk and headed north. Checking his phone, a text notification displayed on the black screen. Quickly scrolling his thumb, the screen lit up.

My place, 8:30!

The name was somewhat less fulfilling than the message. "Marilyn? Do I know a Marilyn?" Shaking his head, Ray hit the side button, forgetting what he'd pulled it out for in the first place. Silently cursing himself, he unlocked it a second time, looking at the time. If he hurried, he could catch the West-bound 82nd.

Picking up the pace, Ray arrived just as the bus slowed to a stop. He hated public transportation, but it was one of the few ways to ensure his cover remained intact. He missed the days when he could simply go where he wanted, when he wanted, and how he wanted without giving it a second thought.

Watching the traffic go by, Ray waited patiently, setting beside a man that smelled of urine. Sighing, he spotted his destination ahead. He stood and made for the front of the bus. It slowed, and the doors opened. Ray stepped out and entered a tall parking garage. It was one of the few secured parking spaces available in this part of town. He wasn't about to leave his car unattended in a public lot. Making his way into the elevator, he rode to the twelfth story. The concrete and steel structure felt ominous. It was dimly lit. The open space and parked cars made him feel as if he was all alone. In some capacities that was nice. In others, not so much. Finding his Maserati, Ray popped the trunk and grabbed the duffle stashed inside. He stole a quick glance at the security camera overlooking him. He'd scoped it out before. Every camera was within shot of two others. That made finding a dead area next to impossible. But he paid for their security, he couldn't complain about its efficiency. Quickly changing into his suit of the day, Ray lowered the top and started the car. He smiled hearing the low rumble of the exhaust. Pulling the crinkled Post It from his other pants, Ray dialed and listened to the ring.

"Hello?"

"Scorekeeper?

"What can I do for you, Ray?"

He wasn't surprised the man knew who he was. Even if Katelynn had given a heads-up, which was unlikely, Scorekeeper always seemed to know details beforehand. "I have a new guy I'm supposed to work with. He needs a cover. What can you do for me?"

"William Crumble, Specialist DEA agent. I've got just the story for him. Bring him by The Palm tonight, 9:45. Tell the doorman you're there to see me."

"What about payment?"

"Don't worry about it. The cover's for the new guy. I'll collect from him."

An audible click came across the line, ending their conversation.

The Pandora Gambit

Levi Samuel

Chapter 4
Drinks on the House

Evening traffic left something to be desired. It could have been everyone heading home after work. Or it could simply be that most people had no clue how to drive. Whichever the case, one thing was certain. He'd waited long enough.

Ray revved the engine and shifted to first. Letting out on the clutch, he cranked the wheel and edged out of rush hour traffic. Correcting into the turning lane, the tires squealed as he shifted again, whipping around the corner. He didn't mind making Crumble wait a little, but to be excessively late wouldn't speak well toward his character. Glancing at the time, he had less than six minutes to make the eight-mile drive. That was do-able. Whipping around cars, cutting through alleyways, and the occasional ignored red light, Ray was upon the coffee shop in no time at all. It was a small place, but one of the best in the area. Sliding to a stop, he saw Crumble waiting impatiently outside the doors. His irritated expression delivered a slight bit of joy. Opening the door, Ray stepped out and marched into the shop, talking as he went. "Glad you could make it. Come on. Let's grab a drink."

Crum glared his annoyance at the human. First, he abandoned him at the police station. And now he was wasting more time by grabbing coffee. Shaking his head, Crum turned and followed him inside.

Fortune smiled on him. The line wasn't very long. Approaching the counter, Ray studied the menu, ignoring the barista. He'd had his eye on the woman that worked here in the mornings, but this guy was middle-aged and a little heavy in the midsection. It was nothing against him personally, he just didn't care to watch the way his body moved when he walked. "I'll have a triple iced latte, whipped coconut milk, honey, and a dash of cinnamon." Ray pulled the money clip from the inside pocket of his jacket. Drawing a twenty from the center fold, he handed it over. "Oh, Crumble, what do you want?" He'd thought about stiffing the agent with the bill, but this was his favorite shop. There was no sense in risking a bad reputation.

Crum approached the bar, glanced around, and settled. "I'll take a large coffee, black."

The barista quickly made change, handed it back to Ray, and went to work. A moment later he handed two to-go cups over the counter.

Ray grabbed his coffee and picked out his favorite seat. It was a chocolate brown recliner with a tear in the left arm. Setting the full cup on the side table, he got comfortable in the recliner.

The only open seat near the detective was a broken-down couch resting directly across the multi-colored rug and ring stained, wooden table. It looked as if it could have been removed from the garbage that morning. Sighing his discontent, Crum plopped down feeling the springs threaten retaliation. He only hoped there were no insects living in the couch. Removing the lid, he sipped the dark liquid and leaned against the puke-green backrest. "What's the plan?"

Carefully swishing the cup to ensure all the ingredients were equally mixed, Ray crossed one leg over the other and glanced at the large man on the undersized couch. He couldn't have planned such humiliation if he'd tried. "We have a meeting tonight. You'll need to dress nice. What's the thread count in your best suit?"

"Um—eighty?" Crum answered, having no clue what he was asking about.

"See, this is the stuff I'm talking about. How are you supposed to convince anyone you belong if you can't even understand the lingo? Come on. We've got some time to kill. Let's go see about getting you an education." Ray jumped up, ready to go.

"We don't have time. We need to find who's running the drugs and follow them back to the source. How do you ever get anything done like this? Coffee, waiting on phone calls, talking thread count. Where are the real cops?"

Suddenly serious, Ray stepped close so only Crumble could hear him. "You need to button that shit up right now. I have a cover to maintain and if you want to risk my safety by raising your voice with such statements, I'll take you back to the station. The shit I face out here every day is ten times worse than anything I saw in the sandbox. It may be slow paced for you fed types, oh so talented at delegating orders to those perceived less than you. You need to understand that the shit outside that door is real. If you're gonna play on my team you're gonna learn the damn rules. Cause I'll be damned if I'm gonna let some Andre-sized suit come in here and ruin shit for me. When you're long gone, wherever the hell it is you call home, I'm still gonna be here living in the thick of it. Remember that the next time you decide to yell about real cops!" Having vented, Ray turned and stormed out the door. He was glad nobody paid him any attention. He only hoped he'd spoken quiet enough to keep from being heard. Climbing into the car, he waited to see if Crumble was coming. It didn't make a bit of difference to him one way or the other.

"Good to see he has some balls. Hopefully he knows how to use them." Crum slammed the remainder of his coffee and tossed the empty cup in the waste bin. Pushing the glass door open, he stepped out, seeing Ray in the car. Nodding his understanding, Crum walked around and climbed into the passenger's seat.

Wind blew across the open top, whipping their hair in the fading sunlight. The drive along the beach was beautiful. The orange sun skimmed the ocean, highlighting the magnitude of gorgeous women in the sand. Bikini's and bodies could be seen for miles. A catchy song came on the radio, blaring through the speakers.

Ray knew it was a Top-Forty hit. That was all this station played. Most days it was the same handful of songs over and over again, as if they were trying to ensure everyone had grown tired of them before they moved on to another few songs. It was a good thing all the stations had gone digital. If they hadn't, there was a good chance they would have worn out the tracks by now. And when the DJ changed, they started the same playlist all over again. Shaking his growing frustration away, Ray turned up the radio, listening to the beat that reminded him of the sixties. Or sounded like a beat from the sixties anyway, since he couldn't recall it firsthand.

Crum bobbed his head to the tune. He had no clue who was singing, but the voice was smooth, and the lyrics were amazing. He wore a new suit jacket. It had a Super-150 thread count, the tailor told him. It was comfortable and allowed air flow, which was nice. But it was still just a suit. He looked good in it, sure. But its primary function was to cover his body. He could achieve that with a ten-dollar suit or a thousand-dollar suit. It made no difference to him. Looking toward the setting sun, he felt at peace for the first time since arrival.

"So, when we get to The Palm, you're going to have to play it cool. Score Keeper is a player. He may test you. But don't worry about him. Information is his forte. He's loyal to us. Just let me do the talking."

"We all have our own strengths to play." Crum smiled, making his own version of a joke against the wordy detective.

Night fell, and the city came alive. Pulling to the front door of The Palm, a line stretched down the sidewalk and around the corner. This was the place to be for people with too much money and too little personal boundaries. But it was far from the top joint in the city.

Ray stopped the car and climbed out. He handed the keys and a hundred-dollar bill to the valet, ensuring his baby was well taken care of. Approaching the head of the line, the greeter stood nearly as tall as Crumble. His dark complexion stood out against the white suit encasing him. "What's up, Marcus? I need to see the man upstairs."

"I'm afraid you're gonna need a different type of venue for that. Perhaps on Sunday if you catch my drift. But if you can settle for a short guy that likes to think he knows everything, go on in. You know where to find him." Marcus unhooked the rope and allowed the regular through. Seeing the large man on his heels, he placed his hand against the brute's chest, stopping him.

Ray reached the doors, hearing the thumping music within. Pausing, he weighed his options. There was nothing stopping him from going inside and leaving Crumble out here to wait. But they'd also had somewhat of an understanding in the past few hours. Closing his eyes for a moment, Ray spun around and approached the bouncer a second time. "He's with me, Marcus."

"Sure thing, my man. If Ray says you're cool, you're cool!"

Crum nodded to the doorman, noticing the earbud tucked just inside. If he had to guess, someone was watching the cameras, telling the large human who to admit, and who to deny. Following Ray, they passed through the doors and stepped into another world. People crowded from the door, all the way across to the bar. Despite the numerous lights flashing and dancing about, it was relatively dark, but not so dark as to hinder sight. Not that such a thing would bother him in the first place. Though he was certain the lights would keep his eyes from adjusting properly. The music was unlike anything he'd consider music. Instead of lyrics and catchy beats, this, whatever it was, sounded electronic. It was a series of beeps and pulsing tones, strung together with some percussion. But people seemed to be enjoying it. As least until they say him. The few that took the time to acknowledge him seemed to move away. As if they feared him. Glancing around, there was more to this place than met the eye. Crum counted at least twelve armed guards placed throughout. He wouldn't have seen them if he wasn't looking. That suggested there was something less than sanctioned going on here.

Ray pressed his way through the crowd, making sure his jacket never opened enough to display his gun. Last thing he wanted was to make a scene. Reaching the counter, he signaled the bartender, gesturing toward the back. "I need to see Score Keeper."

The young man wore a white shirt and an open vest that sparkled in the dancing lights. His head was shaved on both sides, but the lengthened hair in the center was combed into an offset peak. Looking the man over, he nodded his approval and pressed the button under the counter.

Rounding the bar, Ray pushed the magnetic doors open and stepped through.

The tiled floor was polished in a black and white checkered pattern. The wall mimicked the texture of palm trees, including the tops of several artificial palms seeming to grow out into the hall. The elongated, green leaves formed a canopy over the corridor. The music continued to play, broadcast through the ceiling mounted speakers. Though it was at a much lower volume in this area.

Passing the staff restrooms, they came to another door. A guard stood outside, arms folded in front of him.

"We're here to see Score Keeper."

"You're expected. He said to waive the entry fee this time."

"Appreciated." Ray stepped through the door and climbed the stairs to the overlook. It was a large, glass room looming over the unsuspecting patrons below. The outside was mirrored, allowing people to see out but not in. Most people didn't even know it was here. The mirrored glass reflected the strobes, making it seem ubiquitous and less like a watchful eye in the sky. Reaching the top, there was a short hallway, displaying pictures of every big artist that had ever performed at the club. Each one had a short man with brown hair and a big nose at the forefront.

The pair approached the double doors, seemingly made of oak. It was hard to tell from the finish, but their design was one of a kind. They'd been hand carved, depicting a tropical island in the sunset. As they neared, the doors opened and a man wearing a black suit with five o'clock shadow and an earbud matching that of the other security guards invited them in.

Four men crowded around a large desk near the center of the room. As far as offices were concerned, this was nice. Not only did it have the entertainment below, but the wall above the fireplace mantle was covered in a series of large television screens, mounted, and arranged to display a single large image, or several smaller, but still large ones. The floor was carpeted in a vibrant red, and the two walls that weren't made of glass were lacquered cedar. A fully stocked bar ran the length, occupying a portion of both wood and glass walls. Yet there was still plenty of room to spare.

One of the men standing guard just inside the door took a step forward and extended his hand. He didn't need to speak. His desires were clear.

Ray reached into his jacket and drew his 1911. Admiring the elegant firearm, he rotated it, exposing the wooden grips, and handed it over.

The guard placed the nickel-plated Colt in a padded locker and closed the lid. Quickly patting down the known smuggler, he waved him past and moved on to the brute. This guy didn't need a gun. All he had to do was get ahold of you and you were done. He felt a ridged item near the large man's hip. Extending his hand, he awaited the brute to hand it over.

Crum pulled his newly tailored jacket aside, exposing the rubber grip on the concealed Desert Eagle resting comfortable in its custom leather holster. A small spartan helm showed for the briefest moment, wrapped by the lettered EDC. Crum had purchased the holster from a small private shop out of Springfield, Missouri.

The guard smirked seeing the 50-caliber hand cannon. It was fitting. Not only was this one of the largest men he'd ever seen, but he was carrying the perfect gun for him.

Withdrawing the holster and gun together, Crum handed them to the guard.

Laying the pair in another padded locker, the guard slid the metal lockbox into what appeared to be a modified filing cabinet. Having locked away the visitor's guns, the guard marched mechanically, toward the corner closest to the door, did an about face, and assumed a statuesque posture.

Ray stepped to the side and waited his turn to speak. He knew better than to get involved in this. He'd had some dealings with these men in the past. Competition in his smuggling cover. While they were a nuisance, they weren't big enough to take down. At least not yet. Their boss on the other hand, he was one of the big fish in the pond they called Miami.

Three of the men finished counting the stacks of cash and quickly tossed it in a simple, yet sturdy duffle bag. Sliding it off the table, uncaring they'd knocked over a lamp and what appeared to be a container of paper clips, they made for the door.

Ray felt their eyes upon him, receiving the silent message. His feelings were mutual. So long as they stayed out of each other's way, all would be okay.

Watching the men leave, Ray shook his head. They were little better than punks playing a game they didn't fully understand. Glancing at Score Keeper, the short man was leaning against the wood top of his desk, looking annoyed.

Realizing he had new company, Score Keeper sighed and allowed his demeanor to shift to one less abrasive. "Good evening, gentlemen. Mi casa!" He extended his hands, inviting them to join him.

Wasting no time, Ray made his way around the desk and plopped into the expensive office chair at the head of the room. Kicking his feet onto the Parnian, intentionally showing a complete lack of respect to the man before him, Ray leaned in the chair and pulled a cigarette from his pocket. Lighting it with a puff of smoke, he never broke his gaze from the squat, large nosed businessman. "What's going on here? I've only seen that kind of money change hands in a duffle bag for a couple of reasons. None are good for you. What sort of deal are you working with DeMarco?"

Score Keeper signaled the guard.

The man broke from his robotic pose and approached the desk.

"Unlock their weapons and step outside. I'd need a private word with my friends here."

"Boss, my apologies, but I wouldn't advise—"

"Do what I say, or I'll hire someone who will!" Score Keeper demanded, standing on his toes in an attempt to rival the taller guard.

"As you command." The guard sauntered toward the locker cabinet, showing his first sign of emotion. Quickly unlocking the door, he removed the boxes and laid them on the table before stepping out.

Waiting for the door to close fully, Score Keeper addressed the detective, knocking his loafers off the two-hundred-thousand-dollar desk. "You know how it is. I've refused to work with em. All of em. I own the hottest club in the downtown area. Tens of thousands of dollars pass through here every night, tripled on the weekends. And when that kind of money's floating around, information comes with it. Everyone wants a piece. When you refuse, as I have many times over, the price of doing business goes up. Paying DeMarco is just a way to ensure no one shuts me down. Anyway, let's get down to business." Grabbing a folder off his desk, Scorekeeper approached the towering agent, gesturing him to sit. His height was intimidating. He needed to level the playing field as best he could.

Crum glanced at the leather couch, angled perfectly to perceive the desk and the unaware crowd below them. It was much better than the last couch he'd been made to sit upon. At least this one was clean. Choosing the central cushion, Crum was surprised to discover the foam was both soft and firm. It formed to his backside perfectly, allowing him to get comfortable. Even sitting, he was still a few inches taller than the informant turned purveyor.

Scorekeeper sat on the armrest in an attempt to gain those final few inches. Opening the file, he skimmed the content as he spoke. "While I was constructing your new background, I noticed a few inconsistencies. But none drew my attention quite so much as the clear trail of information about you. There was too much. It was easy to access and, in my opinion, way too obvious. Almost as if someone wanted to make sure you were easy to trace. That peaked my curiosity. So, I did some digging. Turns out none of it is real. In fact, the name William Crumble didn't exist prior to two weeks ago when a plane ticket was purchased by some black ops government entity. The name has been strung out all over Nebraska and Illinois since '64. But it's all fake. I guess what I'm trying to say is, officially, unofficially, you don't exist. Your name, your social security number, your badge number, even your student ID in middle school, none of them were real prior to two weeks ago." Tossing the file onto Crum's lap, he continued. "I don't know what kind of shit you're in to, and quite frankly, I don't want to know. This is the type of stuff people get killed over. But hey, I'm not even asking for payment. I just want to be out of it."

Crum stared blankly at the man. He needed to proceed cautiously. If he reacted improperly, that would be no different than outright admitting it was all a lie. Straightening his frame, he cocked his head and looked at the small human. "I don't know what to tell you. Haven't looked at my own record. Maybe someone made a mistake somewhere along the way. Hard to say."

Ray studied both Crumble and Score Keeper. He'd used the small man enough to trust his instincts. And Crumble, while they'd come to an understanding earlier, he really didn't know him. How much of his story was legit? Maybe he needed to look into it himself? There was something not right about it.

Dismissing the response, Score Keeper shrugged, refusing to press the matter. There wasn't much information that scared him. But when someone had a background as complex as this supposed DEA agent, he didn't want to know. At least not while he was still alive. After the fact might be a different story. "So, your new background. I fixed the errors I found in your existing one, removed the DEA ties from less than black ops security clearance. And scattered a full work history throughout. Congratulations, Mister Crumble. You're now a renowned criminal who takes head security jobs for the highest bidder. But you're loyal to your patrons. You've never lost a job, and you have a full list of references in your dossier. Some big names will collaborate your story. And others will be unavailable for questioning. Long story short, you're a trustworthy personal security thug who has no problem getting blood on his shoes." Score Keeper stood and made his way to the bar. Grabbing what appeared to be a wine bottle with a blood red label, he pulled a glass from the hanging rack.

Putting his cigarette out in the pen holder, Ray leaned forward and stood. "I guess we need to get you introduced to the local scum and start finding some leads."

"You guys want a drink before you go? We just picked up a new brew today. Stuff's fantastic." Score Keeper pulled two more glasses and popped the cork on the bottle.

"Sure." Ray approached, awaiting the glass.

Crum made his way to the bar. He wasn't interested in a drink. But to refuse could be in bad taste.

Pouring the glasses, a semi-transparent, red liquid swirled into the cup, settling near a copper tone. The faint scent of pink Starburst wafted from the wineglass. Handing one to each of them, Score Keeper lifted his own and raised for a toast. "To new friends and distant enemies!"

Ray and Crum clanked their glasses against his and brought it to their mouths.

Smelling a familiar scent, Crum realized what it was. Seeing the liquid about to hit Ray's lips, he knocked the glass away. It shattered on the floor, soaking into the carpet.

"Crumble, what the hell, man?"

Crum glanced at Score Keeper. It was too late. The liquid had already gone down. He saw the intelligence in his eyes fade. The drug had already claimed him.

As if looking through a fog, Score Keeper saw the brute before him. A calm spread through his body. He was at peace. Nothing worried him. He felt good. Better than he'd felt in his life. He was laughing. He didn't know why. But it was funny. And then it wasn't. The mysterious man before him changed. He was no longer the well-dressed, albeit large, federal agent. His skin shifted from a bronze tone to a dull green. His stoic jawline expanded, adding to his resolve. Two sets of teeth grew from his mouth, parting his lips to give him a slight underbite with the three-inch-long tusks. The only thing that didn't change was his hair and his clothes. He still had that goofy, business-casual, short brown hair. And he was still wearing the same two-thousand-dollar suit. But he was different. The man had become a monster. He needed to get away from it before it ate him.

Crum saw the fear in the man's eyes. The same fear he'd seen downstairs. He knew it was too late. He needed to use it to his advantage. He needed to find out where he'd gotten the bottle. If the drug was here, that meant Wright was here. Crum grabbed hold of Score Keeper. Locking his fist around the open jacket, he pulled him over the bar before he could get away. Wasting no time, Crum turned and slammed the small man against the glass wall. It shook from the force but held strong. "Where'd you get it?"

"Crumble, what the hell are you doing?" Ray tried pulling the brute's arm off the smaller man, but it was like trying to pull-start an eighteen-wheeler. He wasn't worried about anyone seeing. He knew the glass was one-way, but if it broke Score Keeper would be dead.

Crum glared at Ray, silently telling him to back off. "The wine is laced with Pandora." Returning his focus to the pinned man, he asked again. "Where did you get it?"

Score Keeper struggled against the grip. The monster was talking to him. He had trouble finding reason. A golden trickle ran down his leg, pooling on the floor beneath him until it soaked into the carpet.

"Come on, Crumble. The man just pissed himself. Put him down. Maybe I can get the answer out of him." Ray pleaded, pulling on Crum's arm.

Crum growled. He didn't like not being able to control the situation. Sighing heavily, he dropped the man, letting him fall to the floor. "Fine!" Turning away, he marched across the room knowing proximity was a key factor in the man's fear. He could see Crum for what he was. And that scared those who weren't used to seeing it.

Ray knelt beside the collapsed man. "Score Keeper, I need you to try to focus for a minute. The wine you poured. Where did you get it?"

Score Keeper's lip quivered. He was powerless, lost in the sight of the beast. Unable to take his eyes off, he heard a voice in his head. It belonged to Ray. It was warm and normal. Normal was good. "Ra—Ray?"

"Yeah, Score Keeper, I'm here. Tell me where you got the wine."

"Mon—Monster!"

"There's no monster, Score Keeper. You were drugged by the wine. Tell me where you got it."

His hand trembled. Reaching into his jacket pocket, Score Keeper pulled a business card. It didn't have a name, just a number.

"Is this where you got the wine?"

Closing his eyes, Score Keeper did everything he could to forget the face of the creature that had grabbed him moments earlier. Turning to face Ray, he opened his eyes feeling his anxiety fade slightly. "Ye—Yeah. A guy ca—came in about a we—week ago. Bro—brought a sample in. I bought a hu—hundred cases."

"I understand. I need you to stay here and calm down. Everything is going to be alright. We're going to take the bottle and have it analyzed. As for the rest of it, don't distribute it. Keep it here, but lock it away." Ray stood and turned to face Crumble. "We need to get back to the station."

The Pandora Gambit

Levi Samuel

Chapter 5
Rising Suspicions

Crum held his hand out the window, feeling the warm wind against his flesh. Angling his fingers, the resistance gave way and his hand dropped a moment before rising again. The night's events replayed in his head. Why couldn't he get the man to talk? Surely there was something else he could have done. But what? He was certain, had he been able to redo it, there was nothing he would have changed. Crum sighed, dismissing his failure. At least they'd gotten a lead. That had to count for something.

The blue lights on the radio danced to the beat of the music, playing some alternative pop song. Ray listened to the words in silence. There was something Crumble wasn't telling him. He'd saved him from getting drugged, which he was extremely grateful for. But was that enough to let it go? The man beside him had many secrets. And while he didn't need to know all of them, he couldn't shake the feeling there was something important that would make the difference between life and death. Being in the dark was likely to lead toward the latter.

Turning onto Miami Avenue, Ray mindlessly drove. He knew where he was going. He didn't want to, but it had to be done. Passing the coffee shop he'd visited hours earlier, he turned down a side street and slowed. It was late enough, and using the back alley, it was unlikely anyone would recognize him. But caution needed to be taken. Pulling behind the station, Ray parked between two large metal bins. One was blue and rusted, the other orange and equally abused. Turning the engine off, Ray exhaled sharply, relaxing against the driver's seat. He needed to collect himself before going inside.

"What do we need here?" Crum asked, recognizing their location. It was one of the few places he knew how to find without assistance.

Ignoring the question as best he could, Ray closed his eyes, hoping for a moment longer. The silence was deafening. Finally, Ray opened his eyes and turned to face the secretive agent. "We need to trace the number Score Keeper gave us. If we can find who it belongs to, maybe we'll have some idea as to what we're walking into." Opening the door, Ray climbed out and made for the side door of the lower lobby.

The station was unsettlingly quiet. It wasn't that late, and the calls were still coming in, as they did all hours, every day. But most were of minor concern. Reports of hoodlums terrorizing a neighborhood. The kids would be gone before police even arrived. Abusive spouses, who would be protected when the report was abandoned. Convenience store robberies. The list went on. It was unfortunate. But what else could be done? There were far more criminals than police. And anytime police attempted to do their job, people got up in arms about it. There were bad cops. There was no doubt about that. And they were dealt with when found out. But for the most part, the majority just wanted to try and make the world a safer place.

Ray was relieved to see the station nearly empty. Only a few officers remained, filing paperwork from the shift before, or preparing to hit the streets. It was a never-ending job and these men and women put their lives on the line to do it. Ray had the utmost respect for them. He chuckled, realizing he'd excluded himself from their rank. While he was still one of them, he didn't openly display his affiliation anymore. In some ways it was more dangerous. In others it was safer. It depended on the situation. Reaching the second floor, Ray glanced around for anyone he recognized. Captain Anderson had already gone home for the evening, as had Katelynn, though her desk was on the first floor.

And many of the officers looked new. At one point he'd known all of them. But not everyone was made for this job. A few months could make a huge difference, especially on the streets. Finally, he saw a woman he knew. She was young. Early twenties, if that. And pretty, there was no denying that. But he'd never considered making a move on her. Her personality felt like she would be more suited as a sister, if he had one. "Hey, Alice, I've got something I need you to look at."

The skittish forensic analyst slowly approached. Her wide brimmed glasses magnified her bright blue eyes and bushy brows. Her long, blonde hair was pulled into a tail, draping down the rear of the white button-up shirt. She'd probably be wearing a sweater over it if it weren't so hot.

Offering the half-empty bottle of wine and the pen-marred business card, Ray noticed Crumble step into one of the dark and empty offices. Now was his chance to do some research of his own. "Have the wine analyzed. You should find traces of that drug we took into evidence a few weeks ago. And the number on that card. I want to know everything about it. Who it belongs to. Calls to and from. Any text messages. If it's located on a telemarketer call list, I want to know about it."

"Understood, detective." She took the bottle, inspecting the label.

"And Alice, I have a personal favor to ask." Lowering his voice so only she could hear, he glanced toward the office Crumble had stepped into. "I want you to discretely look into Agent Crumble. He's not who he says he is. You'll need to dig deep. Apparently his background is pretty complex."

"I understand, Sir." Alice pulled the card and bottle close to her chest and turned away, heading toward the lab.

Measuring the remaining officers, Ray silently made a wager with himself. "Who wants to do some surveillance?"

A few of the officers raised their hands, glancing around to see who else was volunteering.

"Good. You, you, and you, come here." Ray picked out the most able looking. Two men and one woman were his choices. "I need you to take a forensic tech with you and head down to The Palm. Don't go in unless you see something blatant. I don't want Score Keeper knowing you're there unless it's absolutely necessary. We can't jeopardize this."

Much of the day's chaos had died down in the evening. It was nearing 1:00 am, and it seemed most people were at home. It had been nearly a week since Crum last checked in. No doubt Kel'Gos would be wondering what kind of headway he was making. Sadly, he didn't have much to relay. But Ray was busy being Ray. That would buy him at least a few minutes.

Stepping into one of the dark, side offices, Crum shut the door. To most, the pitch-black room would have been unnerving. But he was an orc. The ability to see in the dark was as natural to him as breathing. His eyes adjusted as the ambience shifted. The only time it was really a problem was when an unexpected light came on. It blinded him like no other. But apparently that was pretty common for everybody. He just figured it was worse for an orc since their eyes perceived it better. Slipping the bulky, rubber encased phone from his inside jacket pocket, Crum pressed the stiff buttons, dialing the number from memory. His fingers were too large for the tiny buttons, but he managed to dial properly the first time. Hitting the call button, he placed it to his ear and listened to the echoing rings.

"Hello?" A sleepy and gruff voice answered.

"Director Kel'Gos."

"Yes?"

"This is Crum'Bul. Sorry for waking you. I only have a few minutes. Wanted to report that I've confirmed the drug is here in Miami. We found a shipment being distributed through a small winery. The human I'm working with is making arrangements to have it analyzed. We got a lead that should put us in touch with at least one of the decision makers. We'll soon have a name. After that, it's only a matter of time until I find Wright."

"Excellent. Keep me posted when you can. Also, I received your supply request. That's a lot of expensive clothes. You planning to move down there?"

"No, Sir. The style here is different than what I'm used to. If you don't dress and act the right way, nobody will talk to you. At least that's what the human keeps saying."

"No worries, son. I've already approved it. Should arrive any day now. I even added a few extras, in case you break a heel, or spill your Shirley Temple on one." The old orc chuckled at his joke.

"Funny, Sir. You should consider being a comedian."

"I tried. They didn't understand my genius. Why do you think I took an office job?"

"I can't imagine. Anyway, Sir. I have one more thing you need to know. This human I'm working with. He's smarter than he lets on. I believe he's grown suspicious of me. I may have to bring him into the fold."

"I'll let you make that call, agent. It's your life on the line out there. If you think you can trust him, by all means do so. But I'd advise you to have a plan in motion in the event he doesn't bite. We can't risk our existence getting out any more than it already has."

"I understand, Sir. I'll think on it and let you know when possible. Goodnight, Sir."

"Goodnight, Crum'Bul."

Crum lowered the phone, tucking it away. Peeking through the blinds covering the glass window, the human was no longer where he'd left him. Crum pulled the door toward him and stepped out. He was caught, like a deer in headlights.

Ray leaned against one of the paperwork loaded desks, watching the large man pass through the door. He felt like a parent, sitting in the dark awaiting a rebellious teenager to sneak in after a night out partying. "Have a nice chat?"

"Yeah. Just reporting to the home office. Told them of our progress and what the next steps are. They offer assistance if we need it."

"Probably best we handle it ourselves for now. Wouldn't want to risk a mole leaking our plans." Pushing himself up, Ray marched past Crumble, patting the shoulder of the man nearly eight inches taller than himself. "Let's get out of here. I'll drop you off at your motel. We won't know anything until tomorrow anyway."

The low idle of the Maserati echoed off the parking lot outside the cheap motel. It was by no means an impressive establishment. You could probably get a room for around eighty bucks a night, which more than likely didn't even offer a continental breakfast.

Ray watched the door open and the suspicious agent disappear inside. That was all he needed. He was raised to wait until his passenger entered their destination before leaving. That way they wouldn't be stranded if something happened and they couldn't get in. Putting it in gear, he slowly turned onto 79th and passed under the interstate. He wasn't tired yet and the club scene wasn't going to be dead for another two hours.

The drive was peaceful. There was something about the nightlife on the beach. It felt rejuvenating. Especially after an eventful day. Ray pulled into a little place just off the beach, called Club Venice. It was a few blocks from the penthouse he'd been set up in. And while he didn't go there often, he knew the place well enough, though more by reputation than intimacy. As far as clubs went, this was one of the cleaner ones in town. That wasn't to say it didn't attract a criminal element every now and then. If anything, it was the perfect place to arrange a meeting. Both cops and criminals tended to avoid it, as everyone knew nothing was going on. When you needed a middle ground, it worked for both sides.

Music could be heard before he stepped through the doors. It resembled a little tiki bar, but such was just decoration. Aside from the open wall facing the beach, it was fairly upscale. Better yet, the scenery was spectacular. The clientele ran just under a five to one ratio. That meant he pretty much had his choice of women. Most of the men filling the room were scrawny and balding. Some wore wide framed glasses, while others sported thick mustaches and little else. And nearly all of them wore half-open Hawaiian shirts of various color and design, proudly displaying rugs of graying fur matted to their chests. They could have comprised the entirety of the seventies porn industry and no one would have been surprised. Though he couldn't judge their lack of fashion too harshly. Their presence drastically increased his odds. Ray was by far the best looking straight male in the place. And even if he weren't, standing within sight of any of them would raise his own ranking by at least three points. And that was lowballed. Did women use a point ranking system? He wasn't sure. Though his system seemed to work.

Scouting his options, Ray's eyes fell on the second most attractive woman in the room. She knew her status. Women always did. That was his secret weapon. There was no sense in going after the hottest one. She knew she was top shelf in her current surroundings. He'd have better luck convincing a nun to live a life of debauchery than talking her into leaving with him. Instead, he'd target the next on the list. She'd gladly talk to him. It was a status boost. She'd use him to rival the woman above her. And that was all part of the plan. Not only would he land this one, he'd stand a far better chance of landing the hotter one the next time he saw her. She'd have to prove her status to him after he ignored her this night. And that was all it would take.

Ray reached into his pocket and veered toward his target, making sure at least one of the creepy men were within her sight. "Excuse me." He shouted over the music. "You seem to have dropped this." He handed her one of his business cards.

"I think you're mistaken. I've never seen it before." She tried to hand it back.

"I'm sorry, but I can't accept that. How else will you call me?" Ray smiled, setting the hook. Turning away, he made for the bar, silently counting down. "Three—Two— One."

"What's your name?" She followed after, taking a seat beside him.

Easy as fishing. And he was the bait. "Ray. And you are?"

"Vanessa. Do you come here often?"

The question was a trap. If he said yes, she'd think him a regular. Or worse, a wolf on the hunt. Which he was. But she didn't need to know that. And if he said no, the latter could also apply. He needed to redirect. "Would you like a drink, Vanessa?"

"I'll take a Sex on the Beach."

"How about overlooking the beach?"

A violent buzz echoed from the ebony nightstand. Ray opened his eyes, seeing the phone dance across the tabletop. A warmth drew his attention. He glanced at the woman still asleep beside him. She was wrapped in the thin, silk sheets, barely covering her perfect breasts. "Oh yeah!" He smiled, recalling his night's events. Sliding from beneath her arm, Ray snatched his phone off the stand and slipped from the bed. Making his way toward the living room, dressed only in his white boxers, Ray slid his thumb along the green circle on the screen. "Hello?"

"Detective, I got the information you requested about that phone number."

"Alice?"

"Yes, Sir. It belongs to Vincent Merlot. He's a capo for—"

"Dominick DeMarco." Ray interjected. Holding the phone between his ear and shoulder, he pulled a pair of white chinos over his legs and buttoned them. Taking a moment, Ray froze, staring out the over-sized glass doors leading to the balcony. He towered over the bay, feeling the morning beams of light on his skin. The only thing that would make it better would be feeling the sea spray as the waves crashed ashore below him. This was the life.

"Yes, Sir. I also wanted to let you know we did find trace amounts of that drug in the bottle of wine you gave me. I wouldn't say any more than a single drop. But it appears as if it starts to replicate once it's mixed with another liquid. I've already requested a sample from the undiluted batch to test this."

"Thanks, Alice. Do you know how the surveillance team is faring?"

"No, Sir. To my knowledge they're still on site but haven't checked in. Captain Anderson signed off on the assignment this morning."

"Sounds good."

"Sir, I was also able to find something on Agent Crumble. He is not, nor has he ever been a part of the DEA. Turns out his credentials are the result of a complex computer virus that drops him into their system every few minutes and deletes the old file each ping. With it constantly renewing, there's no way for their fail safes to lock on before it triggers the breech. Which ultimately makes him untraceable, yet available if searched specifically. I doubt the DEA is even aware of its existence. It was that hard to find."

"In English, please, Alice."

"Whoever he is, he has powerful friends. Like top government or shadow agency friends."

"Alright. Listen, keep this between us. I don't want to arouse suspicions before I'm able to figure out who we're dealing with." Hearing movement from the other room, Ray stole a glance toward the adjoining bedroom. The woman was rousing. "I've got to go. Thank you again, Alice." Killing the call, he stretched his arms overhead and yawned.

"Who was that?" The woman approached wearing nothing but a thin string that passed for undergarments. Wrapping her arms around Ray, she kissed his chest.

Pulling from her grasp, Ray grabbed his lime green polo shirt off the arm of the leather couch. "Friend from work. Hey, I hate to, well, you know—" He smiled. "—and run. But I have to get to work." Pulling the shirt overhead, he took a seat and slipped on his socks and loafers. Tightening his belt, still run through the pant loops from the night before, Ray carefully grabbed his coat, ensuring the gun remained tucked neatly inside. "If you're hungry, there's some food in the cupboard. Feel free to help yourself."

"You're just gonna leave me here alone?"

"Yeah, why? You need a ride to the bus station or something?"

"No. You've got a lot of nice stuff. What if I steal something?"

"Are you planning to?"

"Maybe."

"Please, don't." Snatching his keys and wallet off the end table, Ray tucked them away. Kissing her forehead, he rushed toward the door. "I had a great night. I hope to see you again, Valerie." He closed the door, knowing she'd try to correct her name.

The sound of cars flying down the interstate echoed through the thin walls. It was a simple hovel. A single king-sized bed rested in the center of the room. Particle board nightstands sat against the wall on each side. One had a telephone, the other, an outdated alarm clock. Shaded lamps were mounted to the wall above each. Across the room sat a similar colored dresser, though it clearly wasn't a set piece. An old box-style tube television rested on top, displaying muted infomercials. And beside the dresser, closest to the bathroom door, was a small desk that doubled as a table. It had a single, plastic back chair on a swivel base with five rollers.

Crum sat in the chair, staring intently at his disassembled firearm. The pieces rested on a large microfiber cloth, arranged in the order they went back together. Holding the barrel, he ran a rod through, cleaning the inside with a small wipe that had been lightly oiled.

A knock echoed from the door on the other side of the room. Quickly reassembling the large handgun, Crum slammed the magazine into the base of the grip and rocked the slide back, chambering a single, nickel-cased round. He stood and marched toward the door, keeping the firearm ready for action if it was needed. Removing the security chain and twisting the deadbolt, Crum opened the door.

Ray was taken back seeing the large man standing there, wearing only a pair of sweat pants. He knew there was some muscle there, beneath the cheap suit he'd been wearing upon their meeting. But just how much eluded him until this very moment. The man was ripped.

Stepping into the room, refusing to wait for an invitation, Ray handed a waxed cardboard coffee cup and a small, paper bag to the larger man. "Morning!" He marched past and took a seat in the inviting chair on the far side of the room.

Crum awkwardly flipped the ambidextrous safety on the handgun, being forced the hold the coffee and cradle the bag. Bumping his shoulder against the door, it swung shut and latched. His hands were too full to worry about resetting the locks. Approaching the bed, he laid his firearm beside the walnut colored holster, decorated by 50-caliber casing ends embedded in the leather. Opening the bag, he saw a thick, glazed donut resting uncomfortably in the bottom. His stomach rumbled at the thought. Orc physiology was different from humans in the fact that they were unable to process sugars. That meant he had to be careful what he ate. But he was now in a rough position. Orcs also had a strict code of honor. And while he hadn't openly invited the human, he did open the door. And that was nearly the same thing. Declining a gift from an invited guest was a sign of great disrespect. Begrudgingly, Crum reached into the bag and removed the slimy pastry, realizing now that it was also custard filled. This was going to hurt. "Thank you."

Ray raised his coffee cup in salute. "Intel came back on that number we got yesterday. It belongs to Vincent Merlot. He's a local capo under Dominick DeMarco. It's the same guy those thugs with the money work for. Vincent dabbles in the usual. Drug running, money laundering, prostitution. You name it, he's got his hands in it. But his main interest is gambling. The man runs everything from illegal pit fights to street racing. And he's smart about it. Never been busted for so much as a parking ticket. He has a whole list of big names. Never uses the same location twice, and he always sends the invite out two hours before the event."

Swallowing the ungodly sweet mouthful of pain, Crum took a large swig of coffee, grateful it didn't have any of the crap Ray had had in his the previous day. "If he's that clean, how do you recommend we get close to him?" A deep gurgle erupted inside Crum's gut. Already he was regretting honoring the code.

"I've been thinking about that. As much as he loves organizing the events, his bigger weakness is participating. If we negotiate a bet, we can probably get a line on when the next one is taking place. At least then we'd be able to see who the other players are. We may even be able to bust the whole operation while we're at it."

"What sort of bet do you have in mind?"

A sadistic smile came to Ray's face. "How are you at fighting?"

The Pandora Gambit

Levi Samuel

Chapter 6
Hard to Swallow

The Palm wasn't nearly as busy as it had been the night before. Club life went hand in hand with nightlife. The golden poles and red velvet ropes that usually lined the front of the large building were nowhere to be seen. Nor was Marcus, the doorman.

A deep gurgling echoed from Crum's stomach and his face contorted in pain.

"You alright?" Ray asked, parking on the curb out front.

"I will be. That doughnut isn't agreeing with me." Wincing, Crum adjusted his jacket. It seemed to have shrunk during the drive. He felt bloated, the pressure growing inside him. It would soon escape, he just hoped it was out one end and not the other.

"You don't look so good. Come on. Let's get this over with and I'll take you back to your hotel." Stuffing the keys in his pocket, Ray climbed from the car. The valets wouldn't be in until later. He walked around the nose of the car and into the grand establishment.

Crum followed, surprised by how empty it was. A few of the guards he'd seen the night before were present, but the vast majority seemed elsewhere. A handful of people lounged about, seemingly unaware of the time. A few appeared still dressed from the night before, mostly men. They wore slacks and untucked white shirts with suspenders. Their sleeves were unbuttoned and rolled about their forearms. Most had their jacket draped over a single shoulder. It seemed nearly uniform, which raised the question, why were they here?

A single bartender worked, restocking and cleaning from the night's labors. It was a different man than the one the orc had seen previously. This was clearly the off time, when they'd be cleaning up from the night before, and preparing for the next.

"Crumble, perhaps it'd be best if you wait at the bar. At least until I can gauge how much he remembers of last night. There's no sense in picking fresh wounds if the scab hasn't formed."

Crum wasn't pleased with the idea. But Ray wasn't wrong. The effects of the drug didn't last long, usually leaving their victim disoriented and somewhat fuzzy on details. That was provided they weren't true believers. Still, if the human remembered the encounter, and believed what he saw, it was best not to press. That was the only loophole to the veil. Once a mortal believed in magic, not just suspected, but truly believed, they could see through it. And that was exactly what they were trying to prevent. Too many people were susceptible to their imaginations. Pandora just made it easier. People could believe something they'd seen firsthand. Belief was much harder if you only had faith. Though that clearly didn't stop the zealots of organized religion. Despite his dislike of the idea, he was glad to stay behind. It would give him time to expel his source of pain. "Fine." Crum marched toward one of the stools and took a seat. No sooner than he sat, he knew he couldn't last much longer. Jumping up, he made for the restrooms.

Ray signaled the barkeep and marched toward the rear doors, repeating the path he'd taken the night before. Reaching the top of the stairs, a guard stood waiting, seeming unsurprised by his presence. No doubt news of his arrival had already circulated their coms.

"The boss is expecting you." The guard stepped aside and opened the door, seemingly unconcerned that Ray was armed.

Marching into the overlook, Ray found the room surprisingly empty. The image of a crackling fire raged from the brick encased screen beneath the mantle. He'd never realized it wasn't real prior to now. A strong scent of pine filled his nostrils. That registered as odd considering it usually carried the scent of tobacco. Triggered by the thought, Ray pulled a cigarette from the pack in his inside pocket and lit it, watching the cloud of smoke rise into the air.

"You know that's illegal now, right? Pretty hefty fine if I cared about such." Score Keeper's voice echoed from the wall near the digital fireplace.

Ray turned to find the squat man's face plastered on the large, wall mounted televisions. There were nine screens in total, a portion displayed on each to make a whole. "Good thing I have an in with the cops. What's going on? Where are you?"

"I'm around. I saw you and your partner coming. Didn't want a repeat of last night so I took some precautions. What is he?"

"Who, Crumble? You know more about him than me."

"You're missing the point. He's not human!"

"Are you still high? Look, whatever. Just come out here. I told him to stay downstairs. Lets you and I discuss a few things and we'll be on our way."

"I'm good here. I have eyes on everything, including your mysterious green-skinned partner."

"Whatever." Ray shook his head growing irritated with the man's paranoia. "The money I saw last night. Those were DeMarco's men. And the number you gave me belongs to Vincent Merlot. You're smart enough to know where I'm going with this. Did you lie to me about the money?"

"No! The money is extortion. They call it a security fee. Keeps them from wrecking my place. Now, yes, some of it was for the booze. But very little. I had no idea it was laced. The sample they gave me didn't hit like that at all. They must have added it after I bought the shipment. Or simply planned it from the start. Either way, they screwed me over and I'm not overly happy about that."

"Good. I'm going to give you a chance to get some payback."

"How so?" The image over Score Keeper's left eye distorted, pixelating briefly before clearing. He held an inquisitive expression, awaiting answers.

"For starters, I'm not going to shut you down. In fact, I want your doors to stay open. Secondly, don't offer any more of the laced booze. Keep it locked away. Once this is all done, we'll get rid of it."

"You'll reimburse me for it, right?"

"I could charge you with felony possession and distribution. Does that seem like fair compensation?" Ray stared intently at the monitor, daring the man to object.

"Point taken."

"Third, you're going to arrange a meeting for me. I want you to call Mister Vincent and inform him that a new player stopped by and had some of your fantastic wine. Tell him I wouldn't shut up about it. I simply had to know where you got it. And after a while you broke down and told him you'd see what you could do about hooking me up. Make it convincing. It's your head on the chopping block just as much as it is mine. Understood?"

Score Keeper let out a heavy sigh. "Yeah, I got it."

"Good. Call me when you have something I can use." Keeping with tradition, Ray put his cigarette out in the pen holder on the desk and marched out the door.

"You trust this guy to just hang onto the laced booze?" Captain Anderson's gruff voice carried through his glass and wood office door.

"He's never let us down before. And he doesn't want to go to prison. What's the harm in letting it sit a couple days? Especially if we keep eyes on the place. If he starts selling, we book him. If he doesn't, we pick it up when everything has calmed down."

Ray leaned against the stacked file cabinet resting against the wall. He was uncomfortable being in plain sight at the station, but Captain Anderson insisted on a face report.

"And you're okay with this?" Anderson directed his attention to Crum, stoic and unyielding in his disciplined stance. His feet were a shoulder width apart and hands cupped in front of him at the waist.

"I wasn't included in this plan. Ray knows the people better than I. He was working on a plan to get in with someone named Vincent."

Anderson returned his gaze to the overly relaxed detective. "And what sort of plan did you have in mind?"

A knock echoed from the door. The timid forensic analyst stood on the other side of the glass, patiently awaiting admission.

"Enter, Miss Kendall." Captain Anderson shouted through the door.

"Sorry to interrupt." Alice scanned each one of them before settling on Ray. "Detective Bradley, I got those results you asked me to run. Here's the report." She handed him a brown folder, packed full of paper.

"Thank you, Alice." Ray nodded and opened the folder.

Without word, she backed out of the door and closed it once again before disappearing behind the wooden frame.

The stack of printed paper was neatly organized and coded by narrow pieces of colored tape. It didn't take long for Ray to recognize what he was looking at. Crumble didn't exist. The evidence was in his hand. And now that he had proof, it was time to find out exactly what he was after. DEA agents didn't just show up after a random bust and agree to work with the locals. When they showed, they took over, end of question. That was just how it went, regardless of who liked it. But he couldn't rightly interrogate the man in his captain's office. He needed to do it when it was least expected. And preferably when there were no witnesses.

Flipping through the pages, there were dates and times highlighted, showing similar patterns to Crumble's arrival, paired against other DEA collaborations. While the two tactics were quite different, there was one other in the department's history that was nearly identical to Crumble. That was an agent in 1982, named Mark Kelly. Scanning the file, this man didn't have proper credentials either, though that was before the current system was in place. They could have simply been lost, though Ray thought otherwise. Another name jumped at him. The officer this agent worked with was a Lieutenant James Anderson. Looking from the folder, Ray found his captain staring at him.

"Everything okay, Sergeant?" Anderson waited patiently.

"Yes, Sir. Just a DNA check on a suspect. It's inconclusive. Guess he wasn't lying after all." Ray clapped the folder shut and smiled, looking from the captain to the imposter across the room. Things were getting complicated. He needed answers and soon. Remembering what he was saying, Ray continued. "Anyway, Score Keeper is going to make the arrangements. Once we have a meeting, I'm going to insure he'll deal to us. When everything is in place, we bust him and make an offer to get him to turn on DeMarco. This thing can't go much higher than that."

Anderson stared blankly at the sergeant for a long moment. "And just how exactly do you intend to get him to deal to you? You know as well as I, it can take months of frequent meetings to even be considered for distribution. And that's on the legal side of things. What makes you think any of us want to give this shit that long to circulate. It'll be half way to New York by the time you get your hands on a shipment. Besides, how are you going to get an in in the first place? The way I hear it, the guy doesn't deal with anyone he doesn't already know."

"He can't turn down a challenge. I figured we make a friendly wager. If I win, he puts me in distribution and lets me talk to DeMarco. If I lose—We'll, I hadn't quite figured that part out yet."

"And what makes you so certain you'd win?"

Crum leaned forward. "He was going to have me fight. I'd win. No question about it."

Captain Anderson chuckled. Shaking his head, he walked around his desk and took a seat on the cluttered, wooden top. "I've no doubt about that." He regarded the agent, unsure if his statement was based on innocence or confidence. Redirecting his attention, he returned to the man he had some control over. "Sergeant, I can't have you wagering department funds on an unsure bet. And I certainly can't have you using a DEA agent as your gladiator, capable as he may be. You need a faster, safer plan. Something to nail Merlot in days, not months."

"I'm open to suggestions, Captain."

As if the wheels were already turning, Anderson offered an alternative. "The IRS and Department of Justice are moving on Damion Rodriguez tomorrow afternoon for tax evasion. They've asked us to assist with the arrest. Let me make some calls. If we can pick him up quietly, without it reaching the press, we may be able to make something happen."

The blinding glow of the overhead lights reflected off the bland, concrete walls. The only color to be found was from the man seated at the table in the center. He stared straight ahead, into the dark reflection of the wide glass window.

Damion knew people were watching him from the other side. He'd seen the same thing a hundred times in the movies. He also knew they were letting him sweat. It was maddening, being locked in such a constricting room with nothing to do but imagine what was going to happen next. It was their way of breaking him. How they'd get him to talk. But it didn't make much sense. He was being convicted of tax evasion. They already had the evidence they needed. And while he was guilty beyond a doubt, he couldn't understand why they brought him here. This was an interrogation room. What was he to be interrogated for? He didn't know anything.

A click from the door roused his senses. Sitting upright, Damion watched two men enter.

Ray pulled the door open and stepped inside. He set a coffee cup on the table and slid it across to the man. "I hope you're okay with black. They were all out of sugar."

"It's fine." Damion heard the chains rattle from his handcuffs. Locking both hands around the cup, he pulled it to him and took a sip. It was excessively hot and somewhat burnt, but it was better than nothing.

"So, Damion, tax evasion. That's a pretty unforgiving charge. One I doubt you'll ever fully recover from. At least not without committing a ring of other felonies." Ray studied the man's features. His forehead and cheeks showed stress lines, and the bags under his eyes were exaggerated. Certainly, he'd been worried about the ruling. Anybody would have been. But worrying about and being arrested for were two entirely different things.

"I'd like to invoke my Fifth Amendment rights until my lawyer arrives."

Ray smiled. The man clearly wasn't stupid. Anything he said now could be used against him. But his charges weren't important right now. At least not in a criminal hearing. They were simply the strings that needed pulling. "Relax. I'm not here to make things worse for you. In fact, I believe I can help." Turning his attention to the supposed federal agent lingering just inside the door, Ray gestured. "Crumble, the file please." Laying it on the table in front of the man, Ray continued. "You see, you've found yourself in a particularly interesting position. On one hand you go to jail for up to five years. When you get out you'll be an entirely different person. You'll have nothing. No business. No money. More than likely, no home. I've seen it a thousand times. No matter how well you prepare for it, people on the outside will forget about you. It's a sad thing, but it happens all the time. Or you can help us. We've called in some favors. In exchange, you'll serve a reduced sentence and stand a much greater chance at recovery."

Damion opened the folder and looked through the documents. The few forms tucked here and there were blacked out nearly to the point of useless. But the images said a thousand words. "You're going after Vincent Merlot?"

"In a manner. We want you to introduce us as your new managers. Me specifically. My—" Ray paused. "—friend, here will be acting as my head of security. And since you just happened to be the owner of the hottest club in Miami, what better way to make the connections we need than by bumping elbows with the most powerful men in the city."

Damion returned his attention to the documents. Scanning in silence, he noted the reduced sentence. It would put him away for a little over six months, and include a hefty fine. But it was survivable. Considering his options, he weighed each one. He didn't get where he was by making emotional choices. But then again, sitting in an interrogation room wasn't quite according to plan. "If I do this I'll need to know a few details. First and foremost, where will my reduced sentence be served? I'll also need to know what's going to happen to Merlot, your chances of success, and how long he'll be going away for. For obvious reasons I don't want to piss off the wrong people if they're going to be waiting for me when I get out."

"There's a risk in any operation. But I'd favor high eighties on success. As for how long he'll go away, let's just say by the time we're done, tax evasion should look like a slap on the wrist. And for your perks, only the judge can make that call. But helping us take out the trash will be a favorable credit to your name."

Sighing heavily, Damion leaned against the back of the uncomfortable metal chair. "Okay. I'll do it."

"Good!" Standing from the chair, Ray marched toward the door, nodding to Crumble as he passed.

The orc turned and followed. He'd grown used to the human's desire to speak privately, typically conveying that message with a silent nod or grunt of some kind. For someone who spent so much time hiding himself from others, he was oddly predictable.

Ensuring the interrogation room door was latched, Crum located the detective. He was leaned against the painted concrete wall across the hall. His head rested against the back of his forearm, as he silently waited. It seemed strange he'd chosen that particular pose upon exiting the room. Such a posture suggested defeat or exhaustion. And neither of those traits currently afflicted their investigation. "What's going on? Everything's in order and moving as planned."

Pushing himself upright, Ray spun to face the man. "Not everything. Come on. I've got something to show you." Throwing his weight, Ray half lunged and twisted, making his way into the narrow corridor of the precinct's basement. Approaching the elevator at the end, he could hear Crumble behind him. Now was the time. He'd get answers, or this whole thing would blow up in his face. Either way he was done being left out of the loop.

Pressing the round button on the wall, the dot in the middle illuminated for a moment, going out with a ding. The reflective doors opened, revealing an empty chamber on the other side. The overhead lights brightly lit the generic wood paneling.

Chromed hand rails wrapped around the enclosed space, and the gray carpeted floor was stained.

Holding the door, Ray gestured Crumble to enter. "After you."

Something didn't feel right. The human detective carried himself too rigid. He was tense. And tense meant he was stressed. But nothing about their investigation should have had him on edge. At least not yet. Everything was going according to plan. Or, as according to plan as it could be. That meant this was of a personal nature. And while the human had been reluctant to open up on a personal level, they'd come to somewhat of an understanding. But that didn't matter. Ray was on edge. And Crum had a fair idea as to why. His temporary partner wasn't stupid. At least no stupider than Crum had been when he trusted Wright. But hiding information was nowhere near as major an infraction as Wright's betrayal.

Taking a deep breath, Crum stepped through the held doors and turned to face the entrance, his back in the corner.

Ray stepped inside and turned, facing the closing doors. Pressing the button for the second floor, it illuminated, and the elevator began to move. Holding position, Ray studied his own reflection. He didn't want to look at Crumble when he spoke. It was too easy to read a face during conversation. And this conversation would more than likely require some stretching of facts in order to get to the bottom. Exhaling, Ray prepared himself. "I know you're not from the DEA." He reached out and pulled the emergency stop, forcing the elevator to halt between floors. Now was the time to turn. If the imposter lashed out, it was best to see it coming. Ray spun and looked into the deep blue eyes of the large man.

There it was. Though clearly there was much he didn't know. Such an opening line, stated in a factual demeanor said everything. "You're not wrong."

"I know I'm not wrong. Now tell me what the hell is going on or I'm going to arrest you for obstruction of justice and we'll take this to Captain Anderson." Ray held his hand on the concealed pistol in his jacket. He didn't want to use it, but if pressed he wouldn't hesitate. He didn't know who Crumble was. For all he knew, he could be a part of these drug runners playing a role on the inside, opposite of what Ray typically did to them.

"Relax. I'm not your enemy. Let me ask a question. How much do you really want to know? Knowledge can be as much a weapon as any gun. And I can assure you what I haven't told you will make you see things differently."

"Let's start with who you are."

"My name is Crum'Bul. Special Agent of Tactical Division for the WMD. We're a covert organization that works within every level of government and law enforcement to preserve life as you know it."

"Never heard of it."

"You wouldn't. It's my job to ensure the WMD and its assets remain out of the public eye. That's why I'm here. This drug we're after, Pandora. It alters perception and opens doors that are otherwise closed to you. I have to get it off the streets before it spreads."

"What the hell are you talking about? What's a bunch of junkies getting high got to do with people finding out about you or your organization?"

"Remember how that informant reacted to me after he got drugged? It opens your eyes to things you couldn't possibly imagine. I'm what's called an orc. Some of your literature attempted to describe us but most have failed miserably." Crum shook his head, recalling the numerous times orcs had popped into fantasy-fiction and movies. Some came close to an accurate physical description, others, not so much. But a small percentage of a very select few managed to come anywhere close to an accurate presentation of their culture. Most of the time they were depicted as mindless brutes that made a good villain because they looked scary. But that was all too often furthest from the truth. In fact, it was usually the elves that played the villain role, albeit in a subtle manner, which often shifted blame elsewhere. That wasn't to say all elves were bad. Most were quite likeable actually. But they had the vocal few that openly expressed their greed for power. Those were the ones to be wary of. "My kind, as well as many others, began to integrate into your society in the early Fourteen-hundreds. Prior to that, humans waged war against us, all of us, in an attempt to eradicate our existence. They nearly succeeded. If it weren't for the elves, who sacrificed their use of magics to hide us, I've no doubt my kind would have been lost. And that's why this drug is so dangerous. It allows humans to see us for what we really are."

"Elves—Orcs—You expect me to believe this shit? Like straight up Tolkien? Come on. I can see you plain as day." Ray had trouble suppressing his laughter. This was the most ridiculous thing he'd ever heard. But the brute appeared deadly serious. That in itself was cause for concern.

"No. Not Tolkien. Those were closer to goblins."

"Goblins are real now too?"

"No, goblins aren't real. At least if they are, I've never seen one. In the movies. The things that they called orcs were more like goblins. Unless you're talking about the big guys that killed that one guy—We're getting off topic here. I understand your skepticism. Especially since you have no reason to believe me, and no evidence to support that belief. I expected as much." Crum reached into his jacket pocket.

Drawing his Colt, Ray took aim at the larger man. "Keep your damned hands where I can see them!"

"Relax. I just grabbing this flask." Crum slowly withdrew the stainless-steel container. Unscrewing the top, he offered it to

Ray, continuing his explanation. "This is a sample of the laced wine we took from The Palm. The only evidence I can offer lay with this. Take a sip and I promise all of your questions will be answered."

Ray hesitantly accepted the flask, eyeing it suspiciously. The stainless casing was luke-warm in his hand. "You stole evidence? And now you want me to drug myself?" How would such a thing go over? He saw how quickly the effects took hold. A single sip would twist him, but he had to know the truth. Crumble hadn't done anything to hurt him thus far. Why would he now? Of course, that was before accusations were made. What if this was some elaborate rouse to get him out of the way for whatever nefarious plot the proclaimed *orc* had in mind? "I don't know if I can trust you."

Crum smiled. His hesitance was understandable. Were their roles reversed, he'd likely feel the same way. "I understand your reluctance. I wish there was some other way. But we're pressed for time and I don't know of any other way to grant validity to my claims. The veil is a funny thing. It works on the unsuspecting, hiding us from their world. But someone who truly believes is unaffected. It doesn't hide from them, which is a double-edged sword. Both allies and fanatics can believe. And that can help as well as hinder. But one who doesn't believe can't comprehend what they're seeing while under the influence. Knowing what I've told you, paired with the drug, you'll have the proof you seek. But I warn you, once that door has been opened it can never be closed again. Whether you drink or not, it's your choice. I just ask you choose quickly. And preferably without a gun pointed at me."

Ray lifted the flask, holding the open port beneath his nose. Sniffing deeply, the sweet fumes wafted into his nostrils filling him with memories of sunny afternoons, playing in a field under an old tree in his childhood. "If this kills me, I'm going to shoot you." He tucked his pistol away and pressed the threaded nozzle to his lips.

Crum chuckled. "If it kills you, you're weaker than I thought."

Tipping the flask back, the smooth taste of artificial strawberry filled his mouth. A calm settled over him, starting in his head and traveling to his feet. He was nowhere and everywhere at the same time, connected to the world, and yet cut off from it. It was a feeling of pure bliss, neither harsh nor dull. Fear drifted away, leaving a serene peace inside him. At the present moment, he didn't care that Crumble had lied to him. All that mattered was the comfortable numb throbbing through his body. Crumble—The thought reminded him of the man's claim. He was supposed to see something different in him. Forcing himself into action, Ray searched the small room, instantly finding the brute before him. The man he'd grown accustomed to waited patiently, but there was something more. It was like looking at a dual image. He could see the man. But he could also see something larger—and a dull green. And suddenly, the first image faded to nonexistence. His new aspect was just under seven-foot-tall. His hulking frame was quite intimidating. Bulging muscles displayed through the tailored suit covering his green-skinned physique. Two thick tusks protruded from his lower jaw, giving him an otherworldly visage. "Is that you?" Ray reached out as if grabbing for a mirage. His fingers made contact, confirming his doubts. This creature was really there. He backed away, colliding with the polished doors. He was trapped, nothing separating him from the monster.

"It is. You see now that I speak the truth. I need you to remain calm. The effects of the drug will wear off in about an hour. When that happens, you'll continue to see me as I truly am. Don't be alarmed by this. You're now a part of my world." Crum took the open flask and quickly sealed it. Tucking it away, he pushed the stop switch to reengage the elevator. "Let's get you out of here before anyone sees you in your current state."

The words reached him, but they seemed distant. As if he were submerged in a pool and Crumble was talking on the surface. Ray began to shake. He felt good, all things considered. But the beast before him was too much. It could rip him to shreds with its bare hands. He needed to level the playing field. Reaching for his gun, Ray saw a meaty fist flying toward him. And suddenly, he was lying on the floor unconscious.

Chapter 7
The Other Half

A roar of traffic echoed through the thin motel walls, rousing Ray from his sleep. Opening his eyes, it took a moment to identify where he was. Memory of the cheap room came to mind easy enough. A dull ache throbbed in his head, and his throat was exceptionally dry. Sitting up, he glanced around, discovering his jacket and shirt removed, folded neatly, and laid on the nightstand beside the bed. His pistol rested in its holster beside them. A near full glass of water beside that. Snatching the water, unconcerned with spilling it, Ray tipped it back, downing the entire glass in the blink of an eye.

A rattling outside the door demanded his attention. Suddenly, it swung open revealing the large creature Ray recalled from his last cognitive thoughts. He jumped back at the sight, uncertain if he was dreaming.

"Ah, you're awake. I hope you're hungry. I got breakfast." Crum closed the door behind him and flipped the safety latch over the extending rod mounted to the door. He carried a brown paper bag and a cardboard cup holder.

Ray instantly recognized the coffee cups and black plastic lids from the place he'd told Crumble to meet him. Closing his eyes, he tried to force the visage from his mind, wanting things to go back to the way they were before. Somehow, he knew that wasn't possible. "Wait—Did you hit me?"

Crum smiled, setting the drinks on the table. "My apologies. You were going for your weapon and I couldn't risk you shooting me." Changing the subject, the orc removed an insulated cup and pulled a foil wrapped bundle from the bag. Carrying them across the room, he handed them to Ray. "I couldn't remember all the crap you put in your coffee, so I got you a Cubano with steamed milk. The lady at the shop said you'd like it."

"What's this?" Ray opened the foil, inspecting the skillet browned substance inside.

"An omelet wrap. Egg, tomato, onion, jalapeno, and fresh spinach all cooked together and wrapped around a couple pieces of bacon, cheese, and salsa. I got them from the roadside stand on 5th Avenue. Pretty good if you ask me. Though I had them hold the onion. Too much sugar in it." Crum took a massive bite, cutting himself off.

Hesitantly, Ray took a bite. Flavor filled his mouth, caught off guard by the unexpected combination. Swallowing, he studied the large creature. Never before had he seen anything like him. Except for a few movies, but that particular type wasn't his preferred choice. He was more of an action-thriller kind of guy. Washing the omelet down with the strong coffee, questions filled his mind. "So, assuming I'm not dreaming, what do I call you? You said your name is Crum'Bul. I can see the connection to your alias. But what would you prefer to be called?"

Crum chuckled. "You're not dreaming. Orc names are broken into two parts. The first serves as individual identification. The second labels my generation. You may call me any combination you desire. Though Crum is my given name."

"What do you mean by generation? Like baby boomers and millennials, or something like that?"

"Sort of. Our history stems parallel to yours. Major events coincide as we share a world, obviously. But instead of your Christian method of time, we name the century. Currently we're in Del. All orcs born from your year of 2000 until 2099 will be named Del. As I said yesterday, we integrated into human society in the early Fifteenth Century, Thar as we call it. That was nearing the end of what you call the dark ages. Near the start of that time period, the human empires expanded and forced my kind from our homes. But it wasn't just orcs. They wanted the world for themselves and they didn't care who they had to step on to get it. This led to a bloody war that resulted in the near extinction of my people. Realizing there was no way to win, the elves sacrificed the wellspring to create the veil. We lived in secrecy for many centuries, drifting into folklore and myth. Only the harshest of places remained free of human settlement. So that's where we went. But with the absence of magic, each generation drifted further from what we once were. I am Bul, which labels me eleven generations Post-Veil. That puts me a little over two-hundred human years old."

"You're two hundred years old?"

"A little over."

"Wow. That makes me feel young. Alright, Crum, I know you're here to try and stop the drug from getting out. You said it allows humans— It feels so weird to say it like that."

"Like what?"

"Humans. As if there's more than us out there. Of course, I know there is now. I just have to get used to it. Anyway, the drug allows humans—" Ray paused a moment. "—to see your kind. And you used your connections to learn that it came here?"

"Yes?" Crum wasn't quite sure where the awoken human was going with this. But he had a right to have his questions answered.

"Well, the obvious aside, why—I guess, how did you know to look for it? I'm pretty good at reading people and you seem to have a personal connection to this. I guess that's a stupid thing to say. If it gets out, your whole race is exposed. How much more personal can it get?" Ray stated hypothetically.

"I do have a reason to be here. More than just keeping the drug off the streets. Have you ever had a partner? Like a real partner? Not someone who shows up and suddenly you're forced to work with?" Crum took a seat on the edge of the bed, scarfing down the last of his wrap.

"As a cop, no. I went through the academy and got stuck behind a desk for the first couple years. The old narcotics detective retired after a bad deal. Should have been simple enough. A shipment of cocaine was moving up from Columbia by boat. Frank and his partner worked their way into the scene. Frank was piloting the rig when his partner got made at the dock. They shot him before he could react. Two months later I got the promotion. Prior to you, I've always worked alone. About the closest I had was in the army. Had a few battle buddies I counted close. But people go their separate ways once they hit state side."

"I had a partner. Kilian Wright. First elf I ever called a friend. Orcs and elves have always had a troubled past. A Millennia of conflict tends to remind both sides of every discrepancy between them. No one forgets. And no one forgives. Wright didn't seem to care about any of that. He was a friend from the moment I met him. At least, so I believed. Turns out he was using me and the WMD to steal the formula for Pandora. We got a lead it was being produced and exported from this little hanger in Chicago. The whole thing was a trap set by Wright. He killed the rest of the team and left me for dead. Been looking for him ever since. Things were quiet for about six months. That is until we found out it had surfaced here."

Ray sat quietly, listening to the orc tell his tale. He knew there were bad people in the world. His job forced him to encounter them on a regular basis. But how anybody could openly betray someone they considered a friend was completely beyond him. "Man, I'm sorry. I can only imagine how that must make you feel."

"No reason to apologize. You didn't do it. Wright will pay for his crimes. That's a guarantee. Until then, let's just do what we can to end all of this." Crum tipped his cup back, taking a long draw. He didn't overly enjoy talking about the betrayal. But Ray had a right to know. There was a good chance this path they were on was going to lead to Wright. Better he learn about it now instead of in the moment. Waiting would only complicate things when action was needed.

"What does WMD stand for?" A buzz echoed from the folded pile on the nightstand. Setting the opened wrap aside, Ray dug through the pile, and found his phone. Glancing at the unrecognized number dancing across the display, he slid his finger along the green icon. "Hello?"

"This is Damion Rodriguez. Your partner gave me your number before you disappeared yesterday. The deal's all set. Come by the club tonight and dress appropriately. Some influential people will be stopping by and I have a feeling you're going to want to set a good example."

"Understood." Ray killed the call and laid his phone aside. "We're on for tonight. You ready to be my new head of security?"

"I think I can handle the job. As for your previous question. WMD stands for World of Mystical Descendants."

"Not very inspirational, is it?"

"I don't know what you mean."

"The name. I would have expected something bigger. For instance, we use it to mean Weapons of Mass Destruction."

Crum thought for a moment, clearly analyzing the statement. "When you put it like that, I suppose you're right. Although for what we do, it would seem counterproductive to go big."

"You have a point there."

Ray leaned against the side of his car, fumbling with the ivory buttons of his new suit. It was heavier than he'd grown accustomed to. But it was the best they could do with such time restrictions. Glancing at the time, he exhaled sharply and studied the creature standing across from him. "I'm never going to get used to seeing you like that."

"Like what?" Crum asked, patiently awaiting the club owner. He was already five minutes late. Much longer and there would be cause for suspicion. Not that it would be in the human's best interest. But people were known to make stupid decisions when faced with less challenging circumstances. Still, their need kept the man out of jail a while longer. The least he could do was honor the arrangement, and be on time.

"All green and toothy." Ray gestured to Crum's face, mimicking the brute's appearance. He admired the new suit encasing the beast. He had a whole closet full now, each one custom tailored to rival the finest available. This one was a deep blue sharkskin, seeming to absorb the light all around him. The three-button design slimmed his muscular torso, adding height to his already towering figure. Ray noticed the hand-crafted buttons were made of pearl, the lowest one unbuttoned, suggesting Crum had read the men's fashion magazine he'd given him.

"Give it time. Soon you won't realize how many people are oblivious to it. Just wait until you see an elf. You find me funny looking, you're in for a surprise."

"What do elves look like?"

Crum thought for a moment. He wasn't sure how to give an accurate reference. A memory came to mind of Wright going on a rant a few years ago, around Christmas time.

God damned humans and their stupid lack of knowledge! Every fucking year I see hundreds of these little creatures wearing bright colors and looking like children. 'Oh, I'm a big idiot! Look at my Christmas elf!' They wouldn't know an elf if it slit their throat. Fucking morons need to learn the difference between elves and gnomes!

Crum chuckled aloud, though he quickly stiffened, returning to the betrayal. In hindsight, he should have known how the elf felt about humans. "They look like prettier humans."

Ray's phone beeped inside his pocket. Checking the notification, he glanced from the screen and over at Crum. "You know, I'm not sure I'd be able to do my job without this thing. I use it for everything it seems. Makes you wonder how they did it before phones were everywhere."

"They used what was called a beat." Crum declared, matter-of-factly.

"What, like street cops?"

"That's kind of how it started. Each constable was assigned a set route to walk. Check-in points were usually set at a Police Call Box. This gave them a few minutes to relax and await new information, or relay any encounters. The call box aside, the route itself was called a beat."

"That's a hell of a history lesson. I completely forgot about those old call boxes. Any more you only see them in the movies."

"History to you maybe. But I was there to witness it."

"Another thing I'm going to need to get used to."

Their conversation was interrupted by a click at the reinforced, steel door. Damion came into view on the other side of the threshold.

"About time. I was beginning to think we were going to have to put out an APB on you." Pushing himself off the fender, Ray tucked his phone away and marched toward the door.

"Ye of little faith." Damion opened the door fully, allowing the two inside.

"The only reason I've got to trust you is that your sentence will be greatly reduced with your cooperation. That doesn't inspire much. Besides, plenty of men with less money than you have taken their chances and run. You want me to trust you? Start by ensuring this happens without incident." Marching past,

Ray was taken back by the extravagance of the place. They were standing in the staging area. Three dock doors rested closed on the far side of the room. Despite its simplistic function, the floors were a polished marble and the walls covered in lacquered wood. Sound tests could be heard echoing through the place, but were greatly muffled by distance. Staff rushed passed the small glass windows set in the stainless-steel swing doors. It appeared to be a kitchen on the other side. Behind him, on either side of the door they'd just entered, a guard stood waiting.

"This way. I'll give you a quick tour. People aren't set to arrive for another forty minutes. That should give us plenty of time to get you accustomed to the role." Damion gestured to a side hall.

"I think I'll show myself around. Need to get a feel for the security." Refusing to offer a chance at rebuttal, Crum broke away from the pair. Marching through the spring hinged doors, the kitchen was bustling. He'd never imagined such a place would cater so much food. But then again, this was more than a simple club. This was supposedly the hottest place in Miami. And from the heat, he couldn't argue that fact. Recalling the files the IRS had faxed over, this place raked in nearly a million dollars a month for the last twelve months. That was nothing to sneer at. But it also had to account for the overhead going back out. And serving around two hundred people a night, they were going to be busy.

Making his way into the main hall, Crum glanced to the stage. The band was finishing rehearsal, seemingly just in time for the event to start. Small, well-manicured trees sprouted through a number of round ports in the floor. The perfectly shaped marble wrapped away from the groomed trunks, forming an intricate design. Scattered between the numerous trees, several white clothed tables sat strategically throughout the room. Crystal and silver dinnerware rested in perfect placement, complete with a folded, cloth napkin that had been twisted and molded to form the illusion of an albatross, the name of the club. The owner had chosen the name as a challenge to fate, daring each man to make his own luck. Considering his current predicament, it seemed he'd lost. While Crum hadn't visited many elven vales, this place held a tranquil serenity similar to the few occasions when he'd been allowed inside one of the ancient cities.

The band set their instruments in their respective stands and gathered themselves off stage. They still had a while before their set would start. There was no sense lingering while they had an early invitation to the festivities before the guests arrived.

Crum watched them make their way to the bar. A young man, dressed in nice slacks and a matching, dark colored vest with blood-red tie went to work mixing their various drinks. Crum wasn't certain, but he was pretty sure he'd seen the band before. At the very least, he knew he'd seen the lead singer. Possibly on TV? Suddenly it hit him. They'd been tearing up the charts for the past few years, increasing their already prestigious status. What better way to grow than by playing at the best spot in town?

"Hey, you!" A large man approached Crum. He wore an earpiece and was dressed in an all-black suit, similar in design to the one wrapped around Crum's hulking figure. Though the dark blue held a reflective glare unfound in the black. His freshly shaved head reflected the soft glow of the overhead lights, while highlighting his manicured goatee. "Guest aren't permitted before the doors open."

"I'm not a guest. I'm the new head of security." Crum informed, anticipating the man's reaction. It could go one of many ways. He'd either be well received, or questioned further. Either way, he had nothing to fear.

"We'll see about that." The guard pressed the receiver button in his jacket collar and spoke into the tiny microphone imbedded in the earpiece. "I've got a guy claiming he's the new bulldog. Any confirmation on that?"

A replying voice echoed faintly from his ear. Crum couldn't make out the words but it seemed this man wasn't thrilled with the message he received.

Sweat beaded on his forehead and his cheeks flushed red. Calmly restraining himself, the man removed the receiver and laid it on the table beside Crum. Reaching into his jacket pocket, he pulled a leather case formed around a set of handcuffs and laid them beside it. "Enjoy the job. Tell Damion it was nice of him to let me know. I'll be expecting the payout on my contract within the week." Turning, the previous security head marched toward the kitchen, disappearing behind the swinging doors.

Grabbing the earbud, Crum wiped away any residue stuck to the plastic housing. Tucking both the cuffs and bud into his inner pocket, he finished surveying the main room. It was fairly straight forward. Guests would enter from the main entrance. Staff would use the smaller, easily overlooked doors spread along the side walls. There was a hallway to the right of the entrance that likely led to the restrooms. He'd check to be certain in any case. And a small lobby rested mid wall to the left, where a single glass elevator soared to the upper levels.

The hum of an electric motor echoed from the stage area. It only took a moment to realize the wall was closing, hiding the stage from view.

Crum guessed it would open again at the appropriate time. This place was certainly unlike anything he'd seen before. And from the door prices, he understood why. Politicians, celebrities, and successful businessmen, legal or otherwise were likely the only ones who could afford to come here regularly. Though he suspected a number of them comprised all those titles at once. Quickly finishing his rounds, learning everything he could, Crum glanced toward the balcony wrapping the majority of the grand hall. And a balcony meant rooms. More than likely, that's where the main office would be. That seemed to be the one thing all these places had in common. The rulers always wanted to tower over their patrons, both in status and elevation. It made them feel superior.

The windows wrapping around the protruding wall were dark, but the guard rails clearly led from either side. It had to be an overlook.

Crum started for the elevator. He had no doubt he'd find Ray upstairs. The human got off on the lifestyles of the rich and famous. Or so he pretended. Ray was much simpler than he let on. But one had to get past his personality first.

Waiting for the elevator to open, Crum noticed something he hadn't expected. An elf walked through the door.

Ray made his way through the kitchen shaking hands with the staff. As far as any of them were concerned, he was the new boss. They had no reason to suspect otherwise. The owner introduced him. That was good enough.

Entering the security room, Ray couldn't help but be impressed by the monitors and surveillance equipment. Every angle was covered from at least three different points, displaying every inch of the place in high definition audio-video. A dull roar could be heard from the main entrance, echoing from the line of people awaiting entry. There was no doubt in his mind that any conversation could be picked up and recorded at any given time. Such was good for his profession, when need arose. But it seemed like a heavy breach in privacy. Ray couldn't help but wonder how many places employed similar methods of screening. For all he knew his conversation with Crum out back had been recorded. That was potentially troublesome. But how could he ensure there was no evidence of their discussion without drawing unwanted attention to the matter? Not much had been said prior to his host's arrival. But it was an open admittance of things that shouldn't have been discussed in public. Ignoring the two security technicians sitting in front of the screens, Ray directed his attention to Damion. "Let's say someone was caught discussing illegal activity while on the premises. Where would that surveillance be stored? I'm not seeing a hard drive or anything of the sort."

Damion chuckled at the question. "We're in the technological age. Nobody uses physical hard drives anymore. Everything is wirelessly connected to the cloud, which can only be accessed from my personal laptop or cell. Both are protected by a 256-bit encryption and require a thumb print scan. There is however a bypass code locked in a safety deposit box, accessible only upon my death. But I'm hoping that'll never have to be used. At least not for a good long while."

That didn't make things any easier. Ray had to be sure there were no witnesses to the conversation prior to Damion's arrival. He was no hacker, so getting in that way would be next to impossible. Once he warranted some privacy perhaps he'd have Damion unlock the computer, so he could have a look for himself. Though that was also unlikely. Scanning the screens, Ray found the docks. Sure enough, his Maserati was sitting out back, unmolested. He hoped it stayed that way.

Glancing at his watch, Damion punched in the access code to the sealed door and pushed it open. "We need to hurry and finish the rounds. The show starts in fourteen minutes."

Ray stepped past and entered the long, surprisingly bland hall. It felt more like a government building in this section than a prestigious club. But it was unlikely the patrons ever came into this area. There was no sense in making it extraordinary. They passed through the kitchen once again and into the main hall.

Ray was taken back by the extravagance. Moreover, he recognized the band standing near the bar. A moment of excitement overcame him. He wanted nothing more than to approach and shake their hands. Their music had gotten him through some of his darkest times. But business came first. He couldn't risk letting his guard down for a moment of bliss.

"Hey, Mick. This is Ray. He's going to be running things for a while. I want you to follow his orders as if they were my own." Damion leaned over the bar, grabbing a bottle from the other side and two champagne glasses. Popping the cork, suds spilled from the dark green bottle, caught in the crystalline glass beneath it. Handing the half-full goblet to Ray he poured one for himself.

One of the band members wandered over, extending his hand to Damion. "Thanks so much for having us. I can't tell you what an honor it is to be here tonight."

"My pleasure. I'm just happy we were able to find a time that worked for both our schedules. Ray, this is Adam. Adam, Ray. He's the new manager. Going to be running things for me while I'm away, seeing to some personal matters."

"Nice to meet you Ray." The lead singer took Ray's hand and gave a firm and steady shake. Redirecting his attention to the owner, he continued. "We're all set up and ready to go. When would you like us to start playing?"

Checking his watch once again, Damion glanced to the doors. "We open in five minutes. You guys will have the opportunity to dine with the guests. We have a table set aside for you. No worries about being bombarded. We have strict rules against such. Anyone who gets out of line will be removed without refund. You'll eat. And after the meal we'll have a twenty-minute intersession at which point the wall will retract and you'll be on. If you find yourself in need of anything, talk to

Rachel. She should be around here somewhere." Damion glanced around, unable to locate the talent manager.

"Excellent. I think you'll enjoy our set. I've worked a new song into the line-up. These people are in for a treat. It was a pleasure meeting you, Ray." He shook both men's hands once again. "Damion. Again, thank you for having us." Adam made his way back toward the band and resumed his conversation.

An alarm beeped from Damion's watch. "Three minutes till show time. Shall we?" He gestured toward the main doors.

Ray glanced around, not seeing Crum anywhere. He needed to find the orc and update him on new developments. Those cameras were going to be a bane that was going to have to be dealt with sooner rather than later.

Chapter 8
Trading Insults

Dull, gentle instrumental drifted from the hidden speakers scattered about the place. Ray thought he'd found one so far, but it turned out to be a smoke detector, leaving him wondering where the music was coming from. It was just loud enough to set the mood, but quiet enough to forget it was even playing.

For the most part, everything was going relatively smooth. Damion had retired upstairs, inviting Ray along. Though the detective declined invitation for the moment. He needed to speak with Crum before abandoning him entirely. There would be plenty of time to checkout the office before the night was through.

"Can I get you anything?"

Ray glanced to his right, finding the barkeep staring at him. Mick, he believed his name was. He hadn't been paying attention to his surroundings. How long the man had been there, he couldn't say. Hundreds of people sat at the round, dressed tables, comfortably enjoying their meals. Many had plates with steak and vegetables, cooked to varying degrees. Others had fresh sea food and rice, while some were as simple as a small salad with some unidentified meat knock off. Ray never understood those types. It was one thing to eat healthy. But to replace actual food with leaves and processed meat-like products, he couldn't fathom why anyone would willingly resort to that. Regardless of the food itself, it all looked and smelled delicious. It had been delivered in the most unique fashion. Ray stared in wonder, watching the flames dance from plate to plate. The blue, orange, and yellow hues swirled and rolled together, forming the profile of a large bird that burned out as soon as the platters were dispersed to their perspective patrons. How they'd managed to shape the flame was a mystery. Ray guessed it was probably a mixture of quick burning alcohols around the outer lips that reacted together. But he couldn't be certain. "Scotch and water, if you don't mind. Thank you, Mick."

The barkeep spun and made his way back to his station to fetch the drink.

Ray spotted one of the security detail near the far wall. The man blended in well. He hadn't even noticed his presence until he was actively looking. Accepting the drink from the barkeep, Ray skirted the room, passing near the band's table. They were laughing and joking among their own. Reaching the far side, Ray approached the guard. "I'm looking for Crumble. He's this tall. Stocky build. Kind of dorky looking. He's the new head of security." Ray estimated the height. He wasn't sure how tall Crum was. And even if he had been, that all changed recently.

The guard raised a finger, silencing the man. Tapping the frame of his sunglasses, which Ray hadn't noticed until this moment, the guard pointed down the hall directly to his right, beyond the main doors. "He just entered the room at the end. Left side."

"Thank you." Sipping from his near full glass, Ray made his way that direction. He desperately hoped he wouldn't draw too much attention to himself. Most of the guests were occupied by their company at the tables. But very few people, other than the wait staff were up and moving around. This made him feel out of place. Like he was the center of attention, despite being near the room's edge.

Reaching the hall beyond the main doors, the tension eased a bit. The floor transitioned from bricked marble to extremely soft carpet of a deep red with golden patterns. It felt as if he was walking on memory foam, the floor contouring to the shape of his loafers. Ray noticed a turn up ahead. Reaching it, he followed it a short way to find another change in direction. Continuing on, it only took a moment to realize these were the guest restrooms. Two openings sat side by side on the right wall, divided by a thick column and half wall. The perspective entries wrapped opposite directions and disappeared into separate rooms at the end of their short corridors. An ornate mural was painted over each entrance, one saying Dukes, the other Duchesses. For the type of establishment, it seemed out of place, but the masterful artistry forming the textured words made it fit. Not to mention, this place was designed to make any who entered feel like nobility, excluding the staff for obvious reasons. Such titles would aid in that purpose.

Hearing a loud crash toward the end of the hall, Ray rushed that direction. Reaching the last door on the left, he pushed open the decorated barrier, matching the wall paint. It had been shadowed to make it appear as if it wasn't there. Inside he saw Crum standing over a subdued creature unlike any he'd seen before. It was almost human. Long, golden hair scattered about the floor, and around its face. Its skin was exceptionally smooth, not so much as a blemish marring the pale white skin. Beaming blue eyes glared up at the towering orc. And the blue undershirt and stark white suit it was wearing were wet from some kind of liquid.

Ray glanced around the room in search of cameras. They'd already slipped once. There was no need to add to it. He saw a small black dot in the far corner. It was a little larger than a quarter. Ray made his way directly beneath it, hoping he was out of sight. Searching the rest, he found another on the opposite corner, just above the door. He was going to have a hard time speaking to Crum under surveillance. "Drugs?" He inquired, hoping Crum would retain his cover.

"Yeah. I came around the corner when he was making the exchange. Took one look at me and bolted. I pursued into here."

Taking his knee out of the elf's back, Crum ensured the hand cuffs were locked tightly and pulled the creature to its feet by the center hinge. It was surely painful, but wouldn't cause any lasting damage.

"Bring him this way." Ray pulled the door open, holding it for Crum and his prisoner.

The orc stepped into the hall, escorting the subdued elf.

Ray passed them and turned into the bathroom labeled Dukes.

Crum was a bit confused by Ray choice of location, but followed. Perhaps they could get some information out of this guy.

Setting his glass on the edge of the counter, Ray scanned the walls and ceiling. Legally, there shouldn't be any camera in the restroom itself. But criminals rarely worried about legality. In their eyes, so long as they didn't get caught they weren't doing anything wrong. Unable to see any of the round devices, he opened each of the six stalls, ensuring they were alone. Finding the last one empty, Ray pressed the buttons on the automatic hand dryers. They weren't as noisy as he'd hoped, these ones seeming to be some kind of heat lamp hybrid with a minor amount of airflow. But perhaps it was enough. Speaking quietly, Ray continued. "This whole place is under surveillance. Even our earlier conversation."

Crum quickly thought about what all was said prior to the owner inviting them in. There was a little information there, not enough to worry about. It wasn't as if they'd traded state secrets while standing in the open. But such a danger needed to be addressed. "I understand why you brought us in here. What next?" Crum shoved the elf into one of the empty stalls. He would have collapsed onto the toilet seat had it not been for his superior agility. Forcing the creature to sit, Crum took position above him, ensuring he couldn't get the upper hand if his guard dropped.

"I don't know. It'll be hard to leave to deal with this guy. Elf, right?"

"Yeah."

"We might be able to call someone to take him to the station, if we can get him out the back doors. I'd hate to make a scene and blow our cover the first night here. You said he was dealing. Pandora? Safe assumption that's what he's covered in?"

"Yes to both. When I came in behind him, he was trying to drink it. Ended up spilling it all over the place."

"How's that work? I thought it only effected humans."

"No. It was designed for orcs, but outlawed in 1918 because it made us too aggressive. It's one thing to use rage to your advantage. But Pandora didn't do that. The rage used us to destroy anything and everything in our sight. It seems to have different effects on each race. Take this guy for instance. He's easily a seventh gen. But he feels like a five. That won't do him much good as only first, second, and third are strong enough to overpower me. But he could influence you easily enough if I didn't have him restrained. It also does a few other things for them, but that's not overly important at the moment."

"Htrae eht mialcer lliw sevle fo ega wen a dna snamuh eht hitw edisa tpews eb lliw scro eht noos. Thguan rof si ecneserp rouy. Gniht yalp elttil a gniniart god gip!" The elf smiled proudly, taunting Crum.

"Shut the hell up!" Crum shoved the weakened elf, slamming his head into the separating wall.

"What'd he say?" The first strums of a guitar elevated the noise of the crowd, alerting Ray to the next stage in the evening's events. They wouldn't have long before an audience would find them.

"Same shit they always say. They're going to take over the world and get rid of all the humans and orcs." Crum spit his discontent. He didn't hate elves as most orcs did. In fact, he had a great respect for them. But this type made him question his opinions. It was sad that a few trouble makers could taint the flavor of the entire race.

"We need to move. The band is starting. Someone's bound to head this way soon. Wouldn't surprise me if security was already on their way."

As if his words were the signal, two guards entered the restroom. Ray recognized the one on the left as the one he'd spoken to not long ago. Thinking quickly, he was speaking before he could stop himself. "We've got a drug dealer. Help Crumble get this guy outside and into custody without making a scene. I won't have outsiders bringing their shit through these doors!" He chose his words carefully knowing all too often, security was often on the take. He needed to make it clear that unsanctioned product would not be welcome. That would leave it wide open once the proper connections were made. "I'm going to go have a talk with Damion. Let me know once this piece of shit is taken care of."

"You got it, boss." Crum fell in line, picking up on Ray's plan. Once he got outside, he could make the call himself. This guy wouldn't last an hour in local lockup. He needed to get him to WMD headquarters as soon as possible. At least there he wouldn't be able to bond out before the cell was locked. But how could he make that happen without putting him in the system? If he was processed here, he'd be out before the night was over. Moreover, that'd let Wright know exactly who was here for him. It was too risky. He'd call Director Kel'Gos and let him make the decision. That was the best he could do. "Come along." Crum pulled the elf to his feet and ushered him out the door.

One guard marched ahead, guiding the way while the other was behind, ensuring the detainee didn't go anywhere. Not that he was really needed. The new bulldog seemed to have it under control.

Ray heard a familiar song start. Reaching the entrance to the main hall, the place may as well have been an entirely different building. The walls had moved, creating a larger opening than there had been before. Most of the tables and trees were missing, the holes they'd sprouted from were solid as could be. Ray guessed there was some kind of underground elevator system they were mounted upon. A few tables remained near the bar, giving people a place to sit that wasn't in the way of the dance floor. Colorful lights danced in time with the music, skirting across the patrons just enough to set a mood.

Seeing Damion across the way, near the bar, Ray approached, recognizing the man in his company. Moreover, the most stunning woman he'd ever scene accompanied him. Ray knew instantly she was an elf. Her straight, brown hair wrapped perfectly around her round face, framing its beauty. The tips of her pointed ears sprouted through the elegant locks, pierced multiple times as far as he could see. Her shimmering, red dress was form fitted to her hourglass figure, leaving little to the imagination, though granting enough mystery to peak sultry seduction.

"Ah, Ray, I was hoping I'd find you. Ray, this is Vincent Merlot. Vince, this is my new manager."

"Pleasure to meet you." Vincent shook the man's hand, silently sizing him. He had a firm grip, and he refused to advert his gaze during their introduction. That suggested he was capable of standing his ground when challenged. He was also dashing in a playboy sort of way. He'd certainly have no difficultly gaining the attention of attractive women. If only he had the money to back it up. The suit he wore, while nice, was valued at just over two-grand. That was nothing to his own collection, the cheapest setting him back just over five.

"The pleasure's all mine, Mister Merlot. I've been hoping to meet you. I was at The Palm nearly a week ago when I had some on the finest wine I've ever tasted. I was led to believe that you were the purveyor of such exquisite taste, second only to your lady friend here." Ray shifted his gaze to the elf woman, taking her white gloved hand and gently kissing it. "Would it be too bold of me to ask the name of this angel in our presence?" He released, hoping he hadn't lingered too long. He needed to make a statement, but not one of repulse.

"Mireya." She stated flatly, clearly unimpressed. Though this human was far more interesting than the pig she'd arrived with.

"Mireya, be a doll and get me a drink. I'd like a moment alone here."

Seemingly trained, she backed away and made her way toward the barkeep, currently busy on the other half.

Ray suspected she'd be able to hear anything they said whether she was present or not. While he hadn't learned much about elves, excellent hearing seemed to always be among their qualities in the sparse lore he'd found. That was assuming any of it was true. According to Crum, much of it wasn't. Orcs in particular weren't anything like their usual depictions. He only hoped mind-reading wasn't among elven gifts. Such intimate knowledge would quickly complicate his job. "That's a fine escort you have, Mister Merlot."

"Quite. Though I assure you, she's no escort. I don't pay for my women."

"My apologies, it wasn't my intention to insinuate such. I merely meant to comment on the beauty of your chosen company."

"Ah. Yes, she's quite refined. But there's more to her than a shapely ass."

"I'm sure there is."

Vincent studied the man in an attempt to learn his angle. There were conflicting elements to his persona which made it difficult to predict. That would make any kind of business deal problematic. At least until he knew the man a little better. "I must admit I was aware of your desire for business prior to my arrival tonight. Your friend at The Palm sent your regards my way. Though I'm sorry to say, I never agree to any arrangements upon first meeting. Though I'm sure we could come to an agreement in time."

"I understand. I too prefer to know who I'm getting into bed with. Perhaps, if you aren't overly busy we could extend Mister Merlot's access to join us privately upstairs? And his lady friend, of course." Ray shifted his question to Damion, ensuring the club owner knew it wasn't a request but a demand.

"I don't see any reason we can't continue in comfort."

"Excellent!" Ray clapped his hands in success. He'd managed to trap the criminal into agreement whether he liked it or not. Refusal of such invitation, considering the accompanying price, would be taken as great insult. A man such as Vincent would understand this. Gesturing toward the glass elevator, Ray awaited the man to seal his fate.

Vincent stared his annoyance. He hadn't expected a business meeting when he'd accepted the initial invitation. And he couldn't rightly decline. To do so once could result in the loss of future invitations. And the Albatross was essential in closing major deals. Sure, one could be persuaded to make agreements in other locations. But why put forth the effort when the wine and dine technique did half the work? And what better place to use it than the top spot in town? He was feeling trapped. But what choice did he have? Taking a deep breath, Vincent selected his words. "You certainly know how to extend an offer, Mister Bradley. I was hoping to enjoy a slow evening with my lady friend, whom I'd intended to explore at the night's end, sooner rather than later."

"My apologies for disrupting your plans. Another time, perhaps?" Ray quickly cinched the noose. Nobody would refuse private access upstairs. More than that, he'd purposely responded with an open-ended statement. It was the polite way of closing doors without having to honor them and Vincent knew it.

Mireya returned, handing a near full scotch glass to the portly man in her company. "What were you boys talking about in my absence?"

"Nothing much. I'm going to head upstairs and discuss a few matters. Why don't you stay down here and enjoy the band. I'll find you when I'm ready to leave." Vincent gently placed his hand upon her rear and gave a light pat, displaying his authority.

A deviant smile formed upon her slender face. Mireya kissed his cheek and turned to leave their company, her smile turning to deadly warning no sooner than she was clear.

Ray couldn't help but feel that she knew more than she said. Clearly the case by the fact that she was an elf. And none other than him seemed to notice. But there was more to it than that. Her smile was meant to conceal other emotions. It wouldn't surprise him if she had some higher purpose than spending her night with the self-important ass before him. "After you, gentlemen."

Bright moonlight shined upon the fenced lot behind the building. Crum could see the rear of Ray's car to the left, narrowly peeking from the docking bay. Directing his attention to the accompanying guards, he gave the prisoner a good shake, ensuring he was in complete control. "Head back inside. I'm going to take this scum beyond the cameras and have a little chat. If you see Mister Bradley, please inform him I'll be along shortly."

Without a word the guards stepped back through the door and sealed it behind them.

"Come on!" Crum guided the elf away from the building. He didn't know how far the cameras extended, but he was going to have to ensure he was well away. He was fortunate Ray had warned him about them. One incident was an inconvenience. Two would result in negative marks on his evaluation report. Guessing he was far enough away, Crum raked the back side of the elf's legs, dropping him to his knees. Towering over the subdued being, he released him and circled around to stare into his face. Reaching into his pocket Crum grabbed the tiny earbud he'd acquired earlier and studied it for a moment. There were no switches, only three small buttons. And another, larger one mounted on the single fiberoptic wire that ran from the base of the device. He was certain that was the transmit button. He didn't want to press that one. Inspecting the three smaller buttons, Crum noticed the minute symbols formed in the plastic housing, telling him each function. Pressing the button closest to the top, the one further from the others, the blue pinhole near the bud turned red for a moment before finally going out completely. Returning the device to his pocket, Crum turned his focus to the elf. "Do you work for Kilian Wright?"

"Ecaf gip, kcid a kcus!" The elf spat at the orc, saliva falling short.

"Fine. You've made your choice." Crum pulled the thick, black phone from his pocket and instinctively dialed the number. Listening to the recorded prompt, he typed in the code and waited for an answer. It wasn't so late that Kel'Gos would already be gone. And considering the time zone difference, it was an hour earlier there.

"Tactical. State your name and business."

"Special Agent Crum'Bul. Put me through to Director Kel'Gos."

"One moment please." From the sound of her voice, Crum guessed the woman on the other end was an elf. Her speech patterns were too musical to be that of a human. And clearly not deep enough to belong to an orc.

"Kel'Gos here. What do you have for me, Crum'Bul?"

"Sir, I've detained an elf in connection to Pandora. He refuses to speak more than insults. I can't have him in the system here. He'll be out and likely to alert Wright to my presence long before I get close to him. Likewise, I can't let him go for the same outcome. Even if he's not connected, he'll talk."

"Understood, son. Where are you?"

"Working a place, called Albatross. I'm currently outside with the elf, about two hundred feet from the North-West entrance."

"Hold tight. I'll make a phone call. Expect a Miami patrol car in the next fifteen minutes. We'll get him picked up and transferred here."

"Yes, Sir. Also, while I have you on the line, would you arrange a net at my location. There shouldn't be much. But there's enough to create questions."

"How big do you need?"

"Small. They're running an encrypted cloud that would be difficult to access manually. A quick scan should find anything that slipped before we became aware of surveillance."

"No worries, son. Hang tight. The dog catchers are on the way."

"Yes, Sir!" Crum pressed the end button and tucked his phone away. "I suppose you heard all that. Which means you've probably got some ideas about running. But trust me when I say it'd be a stupid decision. You wouldn't get ten steps. And we both know you don't have what it takes to overpower me. So, I'll give you one last chance. Tell me where I can find Wright and I'll ensure your stay is a bit more comfortable."

"Go to hell!"

A smirk formed across Crum's lips, stretched tight around his tusks. "Your choice." His knuckles popped in protest from his balled fist. Swinging hard and fast, the elf never saw it coming. The hit impacted against the elf's jaw, echoing in the night. The frail creature toppled unconscious onto the blacktopped parkway. Relaxing, Crum waited patiently for his relief to arrive.

The Pandora Gambit

Levi Samuel

Chapter 9
Politics

The glass elevator rose far above the crowd of people below. Reaching the top, the double doors opened to reveal a large, private room.

Ray was taken back by the unexpected sight of it all. He knew it would be extravagant. But this was beyond his expectations.

The carpet beyond the elevator's threshold was pearl white, reflective against the subtle lighting. The center was inlaid in oak hardwood, trimmed in gold. It formed a massive circle, easily spanning half the total footage. Upon the large circle four armless sofa wedges, wrapped in mahogany leather, quartered around a stone ring. Fire danced within, glowing red, blue, green, yellow, and every shade in between.

Across the room in the left corner, Ray found the bar. The wood appeared to be a perfect match to the floor at the center. Several fixed stools rested before it, their upholstered tops wrapped in mahogany and perched upon gold-plated bases. Two men sat upon the stools at opposite ends of the wrap-around bar, silently sipping their drinks and ignoring the world around them.

To the right, there was a single pool table, currently in use. The maroon felt was pristine and blended perfectly to the oak rails. The only disturbance was the balls scattered about the table. To his immediate right a small stage sat against the wall, occupying the corner before a large walkway that appeared to be a balcony. A girl, in her early twenties if Ray had to guess, danced upon the golden pole at the center. The majority of her clothes laid about the stage, discarded prior to their arrival. A man sat at the edge of the stage, casually flinging dollar bills at her feet.

There was a second balcony to the left. Ray guessed it wrapped around completely, housing who knew how many other attractions along the way. Along the right-side wall, three curtained off rooms drew his attention. Two of the maroon drapes were wide open, displaying dual benches, one along each wall, and a table in the center. The back wall of the middle room housed a large screen, displaying a bird's eye view of the band performing downstairs. The screen in the other room appeared to be set on some kind of nature documentary. As far as Ray could tell, it was something about an exotic breed of lizard.

The curtain to the final room opened. An older man stepped out, buttoning his pants. A scantily clad woman followed, kissing his cheek as she passed. Pulling a folded wad of money from her barely contained cleavage, she flipped through the bills and stuffed it in a small, leather purse. Passing the other rooms, she stepped through the opening near the stage that led to the balcony.

Ray noticed the wide smile on the man's face. He stole a quick glance at Damion, silently expressing his warning.

The club owner shook his head, knowing the detective didn't like what he saw. But what could he do about it? These people paid for privacy. Who was he to deny them? If they used his establishment to get their fix, it was on them. The price of admission waived him of all legal responsibility. His attorneys did a fantastic job finalizing that little loophole. Shrugging in return, Damion made his way past the group, toward the empty couches at the center.

Ray followed, stepping onto the wooden floor, and plopping onto one of the mahogany seats. As soon as he sat, the colorful flames simmered, retreating below the stone ring. To Ray's surprise, it didn't seem to produce any heat.

Damion and Vincent followed suit, each claiming their own sofa despite room for four people on each.

"What would you gentlemen like to drink?" The young bartender asked. He looked barely old enough to serve alcohol, yet appeared skilled in his craft.

"Scotch on the rocks for me." Damion answered, glancing to his company.

Vincent slammed what was left of the drink he'd received minutes before, and handed the ice filled glass to the barkeep. "I'll have an Old Fashioned."

"Excellent choice, Sir. And you?"

Ray thought about it for a moment. Selecting a drink shouldn't be that difficult. But he'd already had a couple, and needed to make sure he kept a level head while equally appearing to imbibe as much as his companions. "Do you know how to make a Brown Pelican?"

The bartender thought for a moment, recalling the numerous mixes he'd encountered. "Cider and gin—"

"—Over ice. Yes, Sir. Thank you." Ray cut him off. He'd put a lot of thought into a nonalcoholic drink that was both obscure and able to pass for a full strength from name alone. He didn't need it ruined by telling everyone what was in it.

"Coming up." The barkeep disappeared behind the counter and began mixing drinks. A moment later he returned, handing them to their perspective target.

"Thank you, Billy. Do me a favor and have security walk the balcony. A street walker made it in and I want to make sure she doesn't get the wrong idea." Damion nodded to Ray, assuring him the issue would be dealt with.

"While you're at it, could you have them find Crumble and send him up?" Ray interjected.

"I'm afraid I don't know Crumble, Sir."

"Security will know who he is." Damion assured, sipping his drink.

"Yes, Sir."

Getting comfortable, Ray tasted the blend of apple and ginger ale. Glancing around the room, there were roughly fifteen people here other than himself and the two men with him. Most were patrons, minding their own. These men appeared to have too much money to spend, but lacked the social skills to feel comfortable downstairs. Of course, that was purely an observation. For all he knew, they simply enjoyed the solitude of the private resort. It was certainly comfortable as far as he could tell. And there was plenty of scenery to gaze at.

The woman on stage lost her top, slingshotting it at the man before her. The pink cloth landed on his shoulder.

Shaking his head, Ray returned his attention to Vincent. He enjoyed seeing a pair of nice tits as much as the next guy, but this was business. He didn't have time to gawk. "So, Vince, do you mind if I call you Vince? We are in private, after all. Mostly, anyway." Ray glanced around in search of the small cameras he'd seen earlier. As expected, several of the tiny black dots rested in the most likely of places. It made him wonder if they were present in the private rooms as well.

"You can call me anything you wish. Though some names may reflect unfavorably upon any future relationships."

"Understood." Ray chuckled at the possibilities. "Vince," He paused. "I don't intend to take up much of your time. I know you desire to return to your lady friend. As I stated earlier, I'm interested in stocking some of that wine I had at The Palm. What do we need to do to make it happen?"

"I'm pleased you found it to your liking. We're always looking for new outlets. And having it served here would be a great honor. I can think of no better place for it to gain a following. The clientele is far superior to many of the other locations such arrangements have already been made. But also, as was stated earlier, I don't seal such deals upon first meetings. Perhaps you can join me on my yacht this weekend. Once I've gotten to know you, I'm sure we can come to an agreement."

"That sounds excellent, but—" Ray paused, leaning against the backrest of the leather covered seat. Taking another swing of his drink, he arranged his next move. Dealing with this guy was infuriating. He didn't have weeks to gain his trust. Information was needed as soon as possible. And thus far he was grasping at straws. "—forgive me for prying, but I'm curious if there's something more I need to know."

"I'm afraid I don't understand what you mean." Vincent swallowed the end of his drink and signaled for another.

"As I'm sure you can imagine, in this line of work I deal with a great many distributors. Whether it's soda, booze, or food, it's all pretty elementary. Money for product. I'm curious as to what it is that makes you question my offer. In all other circles this would already be a done deal. Which makes me wonder if there's more to your wine than is being divulged."

"I see. Forgive my skepticism, but I've never met you prior to tonight. I've heard your name a few times, which made me do some research. I'm well aware of some of your more profitable exploits, which makes we wonder why you suddenly chose to get into the management game. And since we're having a private conversation, between friends. Frankly, I don't trust you."

Ray nodded his displeasure. The elevator doors opened, revealing Crum in his orcish form. Ray still hadn't gotten used to it. Seeing few other options, it was time to break out the big guns. "Some of my endeavors have been more eventful than others. But in looking at my history, you should have seen that I've never had a deal go south. I'm careful about my business. And as I'm sure you can relate, nobody gets in the way of my money. You don't know me. You don't trust me. I understand. But you've made a dire mistake, Sir."

"What's that?" Vincent asked, accepting his new drink.

"You've offended me. So, I have a final proposition for you. And I assure you, if this one falls upon deaf ears, you'll find it difficult to distribute to any club requiring more than a cover charge."

"Is that a threat?"

"I don't make threats, Mister Merlot. I've no time for them."

"What's this offer you have?"

"As you won't work with me, I will no longer work with you. But there's a solution. A friendly wager, if you please. If I win, I want a meeting with your boss. I'll deal with him directly and ensure product finds its way into the top seven clubs in Miami."

"And if you lose?"

Ray swallowed, hating the possibility of loss. Pulling the keychain from his jacket pocket, he held it so the silver trident was clearly visible. "Out back I have a 2017 Maserati Gran Turismo. If you win, it's yours." Ray laid the key on the edge of the stone ring, finding Crum take position behind Damion.

The orc silently nodded his agreement, knowing where this was going.

Ray exhaled sharply. Losing the car would more than likely cost him his job. But he had to make his point clear. And what better way to do that than to offer up a hundred and fifty-thousand-dollar car?

Vincent glanced from the keys and back to Ray. "What kind of wager did you have in mind?"

Ray noticed the sweat form on the man's forehead. His gambling addiction was a known weakness. He wouldn't have exploited it otherwise. "A fight. A man of your choosing against my head of security. Crumble, would you please present yourself for viewing?"

Crum walked around the assembled couches, and stood in full display of them.

"Fists only. First man to hit the ground loses." Ray added.

Wiping the perspiration from his head, Vincent surveyed the brute. He was large and appeared to be solid muscle. But that meant he was likely slow, though such couldn't be counted upon. He would need someone quick on their feet, but well balanced in strength. It wouldn't do any good to get a fast guy that couldn't deliver the damage this behemoth could likely take. But really what did he have to lose? Worst case scenario, he'd make an arrangement. There was no harm in that. Best case, he'd have a new car. "You have yourself a deal, Mister Bradley." Vincent pulled his phone and scrolled through the contacts, searching for the proper name. Finding it, he hit the call button. "Yuri, what are you doing tonight?"

With the exception of Crum, the others sat upon the sofas, chatting between themselves. It was idle conversation mostly, stories exchanged between Vince and Damion.

Ray interjected occasionally, but the majority of his focus was on Crum. He wished they had a moment or two themselves, away from the others. But such a thing would not happen until they left the property. And judging by the current state of affairs, if Crum wasn't up to the task, this might be the first and last time for that.

One of the guards approached from the side wall. Leaning over the back of Damion's sofa, he whispered in his ear.

Crum could hear his words.

"He's here."

Nodding, Damion clapped his hands together and pulled himself to his feet. "Gentlemen, our final guest has arrived. If you'll follow me, we'll get this underway and return to our prior engagements."

Ray and Vincent stood, awaiting direction.

Approaching the wall beside the bar, Damion slid a cover plate, exposing a scanner. Placing his thumb over the glass iris, a green light shot through, making the appendage faintly glow for the briefest moment. A seam appeared in the wall, and the hidden door popped open, granting access to the office behind.

The group entered, the door closing behind them.

While the room was much smaller than the previous, it had a certain elegance unmatched elsewhere. A desk sat to the right, seemingly carved from an ancient tree that appeared to have sprung from the floor. It was obvious that wasn't the case, but the sheer design made it feel natural. The heavy glass top rested upon a number of curved limbs, splayed out to support the surface. They continued up on one end, offering several other, smaller surfaces, and even a small shelf near the top. The wall to the left was a massive split screen, displaying nearly a hundred different videos.

It took Ray a moment to figure out this was every camera on site, broadcasting at once.

The far wall was covered in a massive bookshelf, packed full and neatly organized. If not for the limited size of the room, it was a great start to a library.

"This is my personal study. We're going to take a route that few others are aware of. I'd appreciate if the knowledge of this path stays in this room." Damion approached the shelf and selected a mundane looking book with a red spine. Tilting it from its resting place, the shelf folded out, revealing another chamber, much smaller and blandly decorated. It only took a moment to understand it was a lift. The club owner stepped inside and waited for the others to join him.

There wasn't much room in the enclosed space, far less than the glass elevator provided. Ray stood against the back rail, huddled near Crum. To his surprise, it wasn't the large orc that took the most room, but the engorged midsection of Vincent.

Damion pressed the chrome buttons on the panel beside the door, and it slid closed.

A moment later, the elevator began to move, shortly thereafter opening again, displaying an utterly different scene. They were in a narrow corridor that Ray hadn't visited during his tour. He stared into an intersection of halls, each plain and dimly lit. There were six directions to choose from, all identical with a single difference. The floors were polished concrete, bare, save for a series of discolorations at their opening. They were odd in the fact that there were no cognitive symbols he recognized, but seemed intentionally shaped. He stole a quick glance at Damion.

The increasingly mysterious owner looked at the markings and exited the elevator, turning left.

Ray and the others followed. There was no question that it would be easy to get lost in this place if one were unfamiliar with it.

Crum followed quietly. It wasn't his place to express his opinions on the complexity of the establishment. Though it reminded him of the WMD headquarters. But even that was a leap. The WMD hid things from the world. This place hid things from its own. Why it needed hidden doors and walkways was a question he didn't feel like asking. But someone had taken the time to plan all of it. That was good enough as far as he was concerned. Though the elven writing in the floor of the crossway caught his attention. It was silly they'd gone through the effort of embedding it in the concrete rather than simply hanging signs. But if this was an escape path, as the message suggested, perhaps they didn't want non-elves, or even those unfamiliar with their writing to follow the directions. Still, it was silly. Each path led to an exit. One had but pick a direction and follow.

The passage way ended at a wall. The only evidence that it went anywhere else rested in an odd dial, mounted beside an antique breaker switch. Damion twisted the dial as one would twist a combination lock. When he finished he flipped the switch and the way slid open to display the dock room.

Suddenly, Ray knew where he was. This place contained more secrets than he knew what to do with. It suddenly felt much more complex than he'd originally thought. That led him to believe it hadn't been built for its current purpose, but something much deeper, possibly more sinister. Glancing at the dial, it held the same strange shapes he'd seen in the floor of the obscure hallway.

Crum rested his oversized hand on Ray's shoulder, smiling a toothy grin as he passed. It was certain there was much to talk about. But it would have to wait until the night's end.

Two guards were positioned inside the door Crum and Ray had entered from nearly three hours earlier. A third man stood behind them, clearly annoyed with the wait. He was big. Bigger than the average man. But he wasn't nearly as large as Crum.

Ray sized him. He couldn't shake the feeling that he'd met the man before. But it was far off, possibly in another lifetime. Bringing himself back to the now, he returned to the task at hand. Crum would be alone in this test. He only hoped he'd be able to pull it off. The human had a thick look about him. His greasy hair was long and pulled into a tail at the rear. His chiseled, square jaw was marred by an old scar that ran from his right cheek to the underside of his chin. He wore tattered jeans, frayed at the bottom hems, faded and thin at the knee joints. A loose fitting red Aloha shirt printed with yellow and white flowers draped from his torso. He was strong. But appeared agile as well. Vincent had certainly selected his gladiator well.

"Being as the prize for this contest awaits outside, perhaps we should settle it out there?" Vincent suggested, smiling his preemptive victory over the challenge.

"After you." Ray gestured toward the door.

Making their way outside, not much had changed since their arrival. The street lamps glowed in the distance, and the moon seemed brighter than it had been. The docks were surrounded by a large, paved lot with three open bays long enough for a tractor-trailer combination to turn around easily. Ray's Maserati sat beside the first open space, half blocking a large, blue dumpster and the stairs that approached the steel, walkthrough door. A tall chain-link fence separated the docking area from a large parking lot that adjoined the side of the building.

Crum approached the car and removed his jacket and gun, holster and all. Laying them to rest on the trunk lid, he untucked his shirt and carefully unbuttoned it. There was no sense in getting blood on the delicate fabric, be it his, or his opponent's.

Following suit, Yuri removed his cell phone and chain wallet, handing them to Vincent. He had a good chance of winning this fight. He didn't have as much muscle as the man before him. But he was just as tall, and easily faster. He just had to make sure he was quick enough to avoid any blows. The man didn't have to be fast to land a solid hit.

Pulling a black, plastic case from his inner pocket, Vincent opened the humidor and removed a thick cigar. Removing the plastic sleeve, he brought it to the underside of his nose and gently sniffed. Positioning the cutter on the sealed end, he squeezed quickly, lancing it. Placing it in his mouth, he wet it slightly and spit out the small bits of tobacco before toasting the other end. In a few moments, a ring of orange glowed around the edge and a puff of white smoke rolled into the air. Leaning against the hand rail of the stairs, he awaited the fight to start.

"Are we ready?" Damion asked, eyeing each of the four men.

They nodded in turn.

"Alright. First man to hit the ground loses. Begin when ready."

Crum stepped away from the car. It was already in enough peril without him slamming a man down atop it. Cracking his knuckles, he prepared himself.

"You sure you wanna to do this? I will not hold back. You be a bloody mess when I done." Yuri spoke in a thick Russian accent.

There was no need to reply. As far as Crum was concerned, it had already begun. But the man refused to attack until an answer was given. Seeing no honorable way to engage otherwise, Crum nodded and braced himself.

The Russian charged, intent on tackling the larger man. His arms wrapped around the brute's midsection, the bony shoulder striking solid into the man's gut. Yuri lifted, hoping to topple the larger man.

Balancing himself in the man's embrace, Crum slammed his forearms against his back. It resounded a hollow thump that clearly shook the charging man.

The blow rocked through Yuri's body, weakening his grip. His breath escaped him, threatening to steal his focus. How anyone had such power with so little motion was beyond him. He had to do something. Another hit like that and he was certain he'd collapse. Yuri felt the thick, meaty hands grip his waist, and his feet came off the ground. The stout man was picking him up. Seeing no other options, Yuri kicked behind him as hard as he could, making contact.

The thick boot heel smashed into Crum's face. Staggering backward, he released the man and stood upright. Putting his fingers to his nose and lip, Crum inspected the blood clinging to their tips. His ancestral rage began to grow.

Nearly losing his balance, Yuri caught himself. He didn't know if tripping would count toward defeat, but there was no sense in taking chances. Seeing the larger man distracted by his own blood, Yuri set his feet and swung as hard as he could. It felt like hitting a brick wall. His fist stung, and he was certain he'd jammed his wrist.

The impact was little more than an annoyance. It hurt, sure. But Crum remembered training as a child. A wooden cudgel across the head was much worse. Orc skulls were thick as a result of their hearty lifestyles. Not that such traditions remained commonplace in today's world. Evolution was funny that way. It didn't matter that battle was no longer a part of their everyday lives. Their bodies retained those natural defenses from the time when it was. Another fist soared toward him, this one seeming much slower than the first. Reaching out, Crum caught the weak blow and squeezed. He heard joints pop in protest, though he wasn't sure if they were his own or the man unfortunate enough to be in front of him. Keeping his grip locked, Crum brought his free hand around, colliding with the man's unprotected face. Blood splattered from the impact, disappearing on the darkened ground. He wondered if that was enough. Would this Russian submit to defeat so easily? From what he knew of their people, their stubborn will rivaled that of an orc. If that was true it was unlikely the fight was over until one of them could no longer move. Though the confines of the arrangement didn't call for such. Giving the man a chance, Crum released him. There was no honor in beating him to a pulp. At least not without the opportunity to redeem himself first.

Stumbling backward, Yuri caught himself against the blue dumpster. He was disoriented and not sure exactly what had happened. A shouting voice washed over him.

"Yuri, you dumb shit! Get in there and hit him. I swear to god, if you lose this fight, you're going to be on shit detail for a month!" Vincent broke his cigar, chucking it at the near defeated goon.

Coming to his senses, Yuri recalled the events of the last few moments. He had to win, regardless of what the capo said. He had a reputation to uphold. Such a loss would tarnish that. Glaring through bruised and swelling eyes, Yuri set his sights. Straightening his posture, he squared off and began to charge.

Crum exhaled sharply. He didn't want to hurt the man any more than he had to. But he'd sealed his own fate now. Timing his approach, Crum sidestepped and grabbed hold of the man's blood-stained shirt, about the shoulder. Locking his grip, he stepped into him, trapping the man's arm against his own. Jabbing quickly, Crum punched twice with his right, before bringing his fist around to uppercut.

Yuri flailed, unable to get a hit in. Daze, he became weightless, flying backward. He crashed to the ground with a thud, unable to pick himself up. It was pointless, even if he could. The fight was over. He'd lost.

Chapter 10
Repercussions

"I look ridiculous!" Crum demanded, stepping through the side entrance of the police station. He had a small cut on the outer edge of his right nostril, and another on his upper lip. But it wasn't his minor injuries that unnerved him. His eyes were nearly covered by an itchy, black beanie cap that was pulled tightly over his head. A stained wife-beater shirt caressed his torso, seemingly two sizes too small, narrowly covering the lower portion of his muscular stomach. Boxer underwear displayed brightly above the extremely baggy pants Ray had brought him. There seemed enough material there to house a family of four in each leg. What made it worse, he was wearing a black studded belt that could have easily kept them in place on his hips. But the young detective was adamant that they had to be worn that way. And to top it off, ten pounds of gold-plated pot metal dangled across his chest with a bedazzled dollar sign the size of his fist at the apex.

"Believe me, I know. But it's the only way to ensure we aren't recognized." Ray wasn't dressed much better, except that his clothes actually fit. He was wearing a blue and orange hockey jersey, though the numbers and team patch had been ripped off long ago. Only the embroidered name of Foster remained. A blue baseball cap rested awkwardly atop his head at a forty-five-degree angle. The bold, white words, 'Blue Crew' were displayed proudly above the pristinely flat bill, serving absolutely no purpose whatsoever. Like Crum, he wore a thick, silver chain necklace, but his was genuine. And the pants, while hanging low, weren't nearly as revealing as his companion's. He felt he should be wearing handcuffs to be walking into this place dressed the way he was. Making his way up the stairs, Ray passed the first sets of desks on the main floor. Seeing Katelynn, he strutted toward her. "There you are. I can't express how much I've missed seeing you lately. When are you going to join me for dinner?"

Quickly scanning his attire, Katelynn suppressed a laugh. "As soon as you get something that interests me." A smile breeched her lips and she returned her attention to the files before her. Shuffling one file, a picture fell out, landing atop the others.

Crum glanced at the picture. It was a man, laying dead in a pile of garbage. His face, as damaged as it was seemed vaguely familiar. Suddenly, it hit him.

"You mean my sparkling personality and dashing good looks aren't enough?" Ray rebutted, smiling at his own wit and charm. She'd be his eventually. She just had to give in.

Grabbing the telephone receiver, Katelynn brought it to her ear. "Hello? Yes, he's standing right in front of me." Katelynn handed the phone to Ray. "It's the nineties. They want their clothes back. And what do you have him in? JNCOs? Do they even still make those things?"

"Ha-ha, very funny. Come on, Crum. Captain's waiting for us." Ray nudged Crum's arm trying to gain his attention. The large orc didn't budge. Following his sight Ray found the picture. "Isn't that the guy from last night? What was his name?"

"Yuri!" Crum answered.

"You guys know him?" Katelynn dropped her playful guise, shifting to work mode.

"Yeah. We met him last night. Briefly." Ray responded, studying the picture. His face was severely beaten, far worse than Crum had left him. And considering the picture, he appeared to be dead.

"He was found in a gas station dumpster on 14th and Miami Avenue this morning. Coroner's report says the cause of death was blunt force trauma to the head. We found a baseball bat in the dumpster with him. Forensics hasn't gotten back to us yet, but I'd wager it's the murder weapon. There was a sticky residue covering the entire surface."

"Why does that matter? Shouldn't it be covered in blood?" Crum asked, lifting the picture. All things considered, he'd taken it easy on the man during their fight. He was certain he hadn't hit him hard enough to kill him. Yet the picture suggested otherwise. It pained him to see the man. While he hadn't known him outside their combat, he'd fought with honor. That was reason enough to mourn his death.

"It's a pretty common technique. Especially in some of the lower income areas. They'll wrap a bat, or hammer, or pretty much anything they can use as a weapon, with electrical tape. Once they've used it, they remove the tape and burn it, most of the evidence along with it. We get lucky from time to time. Sometimes they don't wrap it as good as they thought and blood seeps through. Other times, it's something else that incriminates them." Katelynn carefully removed the picture from Crum's death grip and returned it to the file. "Is there something you guys aren't telling me?" She eyed Ray suspiciously.

"Is there any way someone could have done this without a weapon?" Ray asked, knowing what was on Crum's mind.

"Highly unlikely. That's not to say he wasn't beaten with fists first. He's covered in signs of that. But the coroner said he would have had to have been hit with a wide side of beef at over sixty miles per hour to do the kind of damage we're talking. Someone worked him over good before his death. But that isn't what killed him. Though I can't say I'm overly surprised. Your friend here has ties to the Russian Mob, as well as some local dealers. Which I'm guessing that's how you met?"

"Something like that. Come on Crum. Captain's going to be pissyer than usual if we keep him waiting. Talk to you later, Katelynn."

Begrudgingly, Crum turned and followed. He didn't want to talk. Not right now. He needed to process this turn of events and decide how to proceed.

Rounding the corner and shooting up the stairs, Ray reached Captain Anderson's office. Signaling through the glass window, Anderson motioned him in. Ray opened the door and stepped through, Crum on his heels.

"What the hell are you boys wearing? You look like a couple of clowns that just escaped the circus." Anderson said, taken back.

"Ray said it would disguise us if we were being watched. Which he said we certainly are. We had two cars follow us from the club last night. And another trailed us to the parking garage this morning." Crum plopped into one of the chairs, letting his usually stern demeanor fade. He needed to relax and allow his ridged frame to do what it would for the moment. His stress was rising since seeing Yuri like that.

Anderson started to say something but stopped himself, shaking his head. Lifting a brown folder, he flipped the cover and scanned the documents inside. "I had the displeasure of reading your report of last night's endeavors. Let me rephrase that. I'm thoroughly pissed about what I'm seeing in this report! What is this malarkey?" Anderson's bald head was turning red, but his face remained deadly calm. "You had this man, who isn't even part of our department I might add, engage in a pit fight. You wagered expensive department resources on an extreme and uncertain risk. And worst of all, you disobeyed my direct orders in both cases. I've half a mind to pull you off this case and make you take administrative leave!"

Ray sat there, unable to argue any particular point. He didn't want to be relieved of duty. But what could he do? He had disobeyed direct orders. And as of yet, it hadn't paid off. Not to mention the death of the thug Vincent had called. That was likely to bite him in the ass as well. "Captain, not that it helps matters, but I need to add some newly obtained information to that report."

"What information? Please tell me you didn't wreck the car." Leaning back in his chair, Anderson laid the folder down and awaited Ray to continue.

"No. Nothing like that, Sir. It's just, that guy Crumble fought last night. We just learned he was found dead this morning. If I had to guess, Vincent killed him. Or at the very least, had it done. I wouldn't put it past him to try and frame either Crumble or myself for it. That gets him out of having to honor the agreement."

Anderson sighed heavily. "You're right. That doesn't help your case. This whole thing is getting sloppy in a hurry." Redirecting his attention, Anderson addressed Crum. "Agent, would you mind stepping out for a moment? I need to discuss what I'm going to do with my detective here?"

Silently, Crum stood and made his way outside, closing the door behind him.

Waiting for the door to latch, Anderson stared at Ray in silence, considering his options. "I'm not going to suspend you. Not yet. But these games need to stop. I can't have one of my detectives out there tearing up the city like one of the men he's trying to catch. The DA would be all over me if stuff—" Anderson held up the folder once again. "– like this get out. I need you to use your head and make smart decisions. I can't deny that you get results. But the price of those results is too high sometimes."

"I understand, Sir."

"And for the love of god, quit using your partner as a personal meat shield, however temporary he might be."

A chuckle escaped Ray. Quickly buttoning himself up, he nodded. "Yes, Sir."

"Okay. So, on to business." Anderson raised his hand and signaled Crum to return.

The orc sauntered back into the office and retook his seat, his ridged posture returned upon reentry.

"This guy you dealt with last night. Vincent Merlot?"

"Yes, Sir." Ray affirmed.

Leaning back in his chair, Anderson exhaled sharply. He appeared as if a weight rested atop of him. "I want you boys to be careful. I've been in this game a long time. While the players may have changed, the rules are still the same. From what I know about this Vincent guy, he doesn't like being made the fool. And after last night's antics, that's exactly what you boys accomplished. You watch your backs. Even if he upholds his end, you can guarantee he's going to want some payback somewhere along the way. I've had to drape Old Glory across too many coffins. Let's keep our eyes open and delay that a while longer shall we."

"We'll be careful, Sir." Ray answered solemnly, feeling a stronger bond to the older man than ever. "You know, Captain, you could always come and watch our backs for us. I'll bet you tore the streets up when you were younger."

"I've paid my dues. Had enough people shooting at me to last a lifetime. I prefer the confines of this office anymore. But trust me when I say, if you need me I'll be there. Now, get out of here and go change into some sensible clothing."

Wind rushed through the open toped convertible, diluted by the blaring radio jamming out the latest hit single. Ray didn't catch who it was by, but he enjoyed the sound. It was rustic and riddled with a country-rock feel. He stared through his tinted glasses, watching the bottom edge of the sun disappear beyond the glossy blue horizon. The music cut out, replaced by a loud ringing from the car speakers. Pressing the green button near his thumb on the steering wheel, the obnoxious tone stopped, and loud, indecipherable music could be heard in the background. "Go for Ray."

"Ray, this is Damion. I need you to get here now!"

"What's going on?"

"Not over the phone. Get here as soon as you can!" The call ended, and the song resumed, having skipped a small section of the chorus.

Ray pressed another button and the volume lowered. "You think he's trying to set us up?" He asked Crum, curious to the orc's input.

"He sounded distressed. The music was too loud and too close to be from the stage, even if he was downstairs. It sounded to me like he was trying to drown out the noise to keep someone from hearing him call. And considering the wall you have him against, it would be stupid of him to set us up."

"So you're thinking a bug?"

"Possibly. There's more to that place than he's told us. Those tunnels last night were filled with elven writing. It makes no sense why they would let one of their strongholds go."

"We could always ask him."

"Do you think he'd tell the truth?" Crum questioned, following the setting sun around the corner.

"It would depend on what's going on that we don't know about."

"Indeed."

Shifting gears, Ray accelerated and shot around a group of cars stopped at a red light. From Damion's tone, he didn't have time to wait for it to change.

Ray pressed the black button mounted beside the rear entrance door. A moment later it opened, revealing one of the guards Ray had seen the night before.

The pair stepped inside, hearing it click shut behind them. "Where's Damion?"

"Upstairs." One of the guards answered, though it was impossible to determine which.

Navigating the large building, they found the glass elevator they'd used the night before. It would have been much quicker to take the private tunnels, but that meant knowing how to open the passage, and neither did. Considering the way Damion spoke, the guards were unlikely to know either, if they even knew of its existence. That was likely above their pay grade.

Stepping inside, the doors closed and the lift began moving. It only took a moment to reach the top floor. There was a noticeable difference in the atmosphere. Not a soul lingered in the private lounge. The girls were nowhere to be found. And the lights behind the bar were out. Through the wall, classical music echoed.

Ray approached the sealed door. He doubted the scanner would work for him, but decided to give it a try anyway. Sliding the cover panel up, he placed his thumb on the glass. The light shot through, making it glow briefly, and then it turned red and began buzzing. The music quieted and footsteps could be heard from the other side. Ray felt a strong sense like he was being watched. Nodding to Crum, he reached into his jacket and wrapped his hand around the pistol.

The buzzing quit, and a click echoed through the barrier. It slowly swung open, revealing Damion on the other side. He looked as if he hadn't slept in days. Heavy bags rested under his eyes. A light bit of hair grew on his cheeks and chin. And he wore the same clothes he'd had on the night before, though now wrinkled and unkempt. Refusing to say a word, he nodded and stepped back inside, so he could close the door once they'd entered.

Ray stepped inside, followed by Crum. The door latched behind them and Damion marched toward the record player sitting along the wall. They hadn't noticed it on their previous visit, but there was a collection of vinyl records taking up an entire shelf beside the desk. An old horn style player rested atop it all.

Turning the volume as loud as it would go, Damion spun and signaled toward the book case. Making his way across the room, he pulled the red bound lever and the case slid open. He gestured to enter.

Crum stepped in without word. Ray however, hesitated. "What's going on?"

Glancing around, as if he had an audience, Damion held his finger to his mouth and repeated the gesture.

Shaking his head, Ray obeyed.

Following them, Damion waited for the door to seal and he twisted the switch to kill the power. The internal lights went out and the small chamber was instantly dark.

"What the hell, Damion?" Ray asked, returning his hand to his gun.

A moment later, light erupted from a hand-held flashlight in the exhausted club owner's hand. "I'm sorry for the secrecy. But we have a huge problem."

"I'll say. What the hell is going on?" Ray was growing impatient with all of this.

"I don't know what you guys did. But my head is on the chopping block now too!" Damion was nearly in tears. The light trembled in his clenched grip.

"Slow down. What happened?" Ray glanced at Crum, wondering if the orc was going to give any backup.

"After you guys left last night. Once everyone left. I got a phone call. It was Vincent. He told me pull to the footage of the fight. Told me to put it on a disc and erase the original. He said he'd kill my family in front of me if I didn't. I didn't understand why he cared so much. It seemed like an awful big threat for something so trivial. But I agreed. I went to pull the footage only to find it was gone. I scanned through everything last night. It was all there, except for two little details. The two of you! Every camera that had either one of you on it was dead. And not like a momentary reboot kind of dead. I'm talking completely offline, unable to connect, no power kind of dead. But only as long as you were in the shot. The elevator camera went dead as the door opened, and came back on when they closed the second time. Every camera on site reacted the same way. I had a complete system test done. There were no reported problems, which makes me think you guys did something to keep from being seen. So, you tell me what's going on!" Tears began to roll down the man's face. "I don't know what kind of game you guys are playing at but whatever it is, you've fucked me. You've fucked me hard!" He was full on crying, unable to steel himself. Sniffing, he continued. "I tried to tell him the cameras were down. That they didn't pick up any of the fight. But he said I was protecting you and hung up. And then just before I called you, my mother called. My sister never came home from school. She signed in this morning, but she never signed out. She's all I have!" He sobbed, collapsing to the floor. Damion covered his eyes in an attempt to block out his fear. The flashlight hit the floor and rolled toward Crum, shining on the wall at his feet.

Picking the light off the floor, Crum stared at the weeping man. He felt bad for him. He'd created many of his own troubles. But this one was beyond his control. In fact, Crum felt personally responsible for it. Had he not requested the net, the footage would still be available. But he couldn't change what was done.

He could only work to repair it. Kneeling beside the broken man, he spoke in a low, even tone. "I'm sorry for what you must be going through. I promise we're going to do everything we can to fix this and find your sister. But we need your patience. We're waiting for Vincent's call. As soon as we meet with him, we'll work out a deal."

Staring into the brute's face, Damion's gaze hardened. "And what if she's already dead?"

"I doubt she is. Dead people don't make good leverage. We'll find her and get her back. But we can't do that if we're locked in an elevator." Ray added coldly. It was never a pretty sight seeing a man break. They usually made worse mistakes after the fact and became a danger to everyone around them.

Shooting a questioning glance at Ray, Crum continued. "You have a club to run. I recommend you shave, and change your clothes. Ray and I have some things to look into. We'll be back before opening. Until then, you need to keep your head in the game."

Taking a deep breath, Damion wiped his nose on his sleeve and picked himself up. "Yeah." He sighed. "The show must go on." Flipping the switch, the lights returned, rendering the flashlight unnecessary.

The Pandora Gambit

Levi Samuel

Chapter 11
The Show Must Go On

"Captain, I understand we have limited resources for this kind of thing. Yes, I know how it would look to take him by force. That's not what I'm asking—" Ray sighed heavily. It seemed his words had fallen upon deaf ears. That was briefly before he'd started repeating everything Anderson said. It was the only way to get him to move on. "Yes, Sir. No, I'm not suggesting we— Okay, Sir." He ended the call, knowing Anderson had already hung up. Turning his attention to Crum, Ray explained, knowing the orc could already guess what had happened. "I got the standard lecture. This is what happens when you don't think before you act. Let this be a reminder the next time—" Ray cut himself off, taking a deep breath. "He's going to issue an APB for the girl. But he said he can't do much else. If he moves on Merlot, this investigation is pretty much dead. Our best option is to force his hand. If we can get him to incriminate himself, we can flip him and find out where he's getting the drugs."

"It's a good plan in theory. But we don't have much time. That girl is counting on us and we're still waiting. You know how these things go. The longer she's gone, the less likely she is to return."

"I know!" Ray snapped, not meaning to direct it at Crum. Things had gotten so complicated so quickly. He needed to find a way out before it swallowed him whole. He needed to end this. "I'm sorry." Running his fingers through his hair, he took a deep breath to calm himself. "Alright, we know Vincent works for DeMarco. We know Vincent has a grudge against us. But we don't know where either of them are, or really how to contact them. We have a missing girl as a possible hostage. And our cover is holding by a thread. If you have any ideas, now's the time. Cause I'm running out."

"As you've already said, we need to force him into action. If we can make him rush, he'll be sloppy, as we've already seen. Sloppy people make mistakes." Crum added simply, as if it was but a minor challenge.

"I don't disagree. But how do you suggest we do this? It's not like we can simply call him to turn up the heat. Sending units after him would certainly get his attention. But he's also likely to kill the girl, if he has her. We need to get his attention without setting him off."

"Do you know anyone who could get in touch with his boss? If we go over his head, that's certain to force his hand."

"No, that's why we went after Vincent in the first place. He was the easiest to reach."

Crum thought for a moment. Suddenly, an idea came to mind. "We don't have to go over his head. We just have to make him think we did."

"How do you recommend we manage that?" Ray asked, unable to piece together what the orc had in mind.

"Simple. Damion can contact him. We send a thank you message. Make it sound like we've already made arrangements with DeMarco. Vincent will either go straight to his boss, which will certainly draw his attention toward us. Or he'll reach out to us himself."

"You might be a genius, my ugly, green-skinned friend."

"I'll have you know I'm considered one of the more attractive orcs of my generation."

"You know all the orcs of your generation?" Ray asked earnestly. That seemed an impossible feat. There was no possible way he could come close to knowing every human of his own. But from what Crum had told him about orc culture, there didn't seem to be a whole lot of them.

"I've met them all, but I can't claim to know them. Most I only saw once, when we were named."

"You weren't named at birth?"

"We're given name at birth, yes. But our generation isn't named until we reach a new age. I think you call it, turn of the century. My generation was named in your year 1900. I was 104 and freshly considered an adult."

Shaking his head, Ray wondered how different Crum's people were from his own. "If you know all of the Buls, how many are there?

"Twenty-nine last I knew. There used to be more but some died in the great wars. And one got hit by a car."

"A car?"

"Yeah. They were still new back then. He thought it would stop like a horse. But it didn't."

Ray busted into laughter, unable to stop himself. Forcing his laughter aside, he pulled a cigarette from his inside pocket. Tapping it a few times on the silver zippo, he lit up and blew out a puff of white smoke. "We should be getting back. I've a feeling we're going to have to keep a close watch on Damion. At least until we can get all of this settled."

"I agree. And we need him to send the message."

Questions swarmed all around him. He couldn't think straight, let alone focus on a single one to give an answer. Ray scanned over the crowd of people, unable to remember most of their names. He met them the previous evening, he knew that much. And some he recalled their duties. But that was it. The roar of their voices was deafening, and the lights all around him were blinding, despite their dull radiance. Picking one of the faces he recognized, Ray spoke, hushing all others. "You! You work in the kitchen. The sous chef? What's your question?"

The man was taken back. It was as if the manager hadn't heard a single word he'd been saying. Concealing his aggravation, he repeated his query, letting his French accent flourish the words. "Which would you prefer for main entree? The Chicken Basquaise, or Veal and Mushroom Risotto?"

"Uh, the chicken one?"

The chef turned and headed back toward the kitchen without another word. It was clear this new manager didn't understand his flair. This was going to be a long battle. He needed to prepare for the man's inattentiveness.

Picking out the next face, Ray settled on a young woman. She was in her late twenties. cute by appearance, but too business focused to have much fun. Her brunette hair was pulled into a tail, and she wore a light gray pant suit. The narrow glasses enlarged her wonderous, green eyes. "My apologies. I remember you. But what's your job again?"

"Talent manager."

"Right. And what's your question?"

She gestured to a man at her side. Unlike most others, he was dressed in a pair of ratty jeans and a black tee-shirt. He wore a baseball cap and a thick, brown beard covered the majority of his face, hanging to mid-chest. All of this would have seemed strange were it not for the hard guitar case slung across his back. "This is Joe Baggins. He's here as tonight's entertainment for the first appearance of his new solo career."

Joe stepped forward and shook the man's hand. "Good to meet you."

Ray paused a moment, his hand locked in the grip of the man before him. Suddenly, his face, more aptly, his beard rang into memory. "Weren't you the drummer for Shaman's Harvest?"

"At one point in time." Joe changed the subject, hoping to focus on the future. "Tonight, I'm thinking I'll break out a couple new originals. Then, depending on the crowd, I may toss in an old one."

"You're the professional. Do what you think is best. Have—" Ray froze, regarding the woman. "I'm sorry, what was your name again?"

"Rachel!" She insisted.

"Thank you. Have Rachel here show you to the stage, so you can get a feel. If memory serves, you'll get to partake of the festivities before your set starts. I'm sure Rachel can set you up with an itinerary. It was a pleasure to meet you, Joe. And good luck in your career."

"Thank you." The singer-songwriter turned and followed the woman toward the far wall, seeming amazed by the setup.

"Next!" Ray ordered, wondering where the hell Damion was. He hadn't seen him since the outburst in the elevator hours earlier.

Watching people saunter through the door, being escorted to their various tables by the staff, Crum stood off to the side. So far, he'd seen two elves among the numerous humans. But they didn't appear to be anything other than patrons. In truth, all he really could do was stand around and watch. The security team was exceptionally good at their jobs. They'd developed a working routine. He saw no reason to change it. Though some of its members he didn't care for. But this wasn't his real job. So long as they didn't do anything too outrageous, he wouldn't hamper them. Voices echoed from the piece, tucked neatly inside his ear.

"We've got a disturbance out front. Looks like two guys arguing over a girl."

Crum recalled the list of names, their duties, and positions. Pressing the concealed button on the collar of his jacket, he spoke quietly as not to draw attention in the crowding room. "Thompson and Stevens, check it out. If it appears to be an ongoing thing, turn them all away."

"On it!" A voice answered.

Crum scanned the room once again. This was going to get old fast. Seeing Ray near the kitchen, he made his way closer. There was still a steady flow of people approaching him. The young human appeared worn from the constant barrage.

"No! I said gray cloth, yellow flowers. Not yellow cloth, gray flowers. Do they even make gray flowers?" Ray's hands moved excessively, in a feeble attempt to express his intention. "You know what, just—go. Figure it out." Looking around, he exhaled sharply. "Has anyone seen Damion?"

His question was met with silence. The young man holding the yellow cloth napkins rushed back into the kitchen, disappearing behind the seemingly constant swinging doors.

"How's it going?" Crum asked, stepping into the thinning crowd of people in search of answers.

"I haven't had a minute to myself since we got here. Have you seen Damion anywhere?"

"Not since earlier. You want me to find him?"

"Anderson called. The girl's been found. She snuck out of school and left with a boy. They found them parked at Hobie Beach. I'm sure he'd want to know. To tell you the truth, I don't know how he deals with this night after night."

"I'm sure much of it is a lack of familiarity. They're not familiar with you, nor you them. And you're here to make a change. They just want someone to tell them what to do." Crum explained with a wisdom Ray always forgot the orc had.

"This is why I don't work with people. Nobody wants to take initiative anymore."

"Most are afraid of getting their ass chewed for making a decision above their pay grade."

"You sound like one who's worked for too many micromanagers."

"We'll, we all had our fast-food jobs at one point or another. Mine were just later in life"

"You worked fast-food?" Ray chuckled, imagining the orc wearing a white paper hat and an apron.

"It was a long time ago in California. I worked at this new place called A&W. It stood for Allen and Wright. Mister Allen is the one that hired me, but Mister Wright is the one who trained me. I didn't know it then, but Mister Wright was the grandfather to—" Crum withdrew into silence. He hated when his mind went back to Wright. "But I think they still make soda." He added. "I'm gonna go find Damion."

"Alright." Ray watched him wander off. Part of him felt bad for the orc. He'd never had a partner long enough to feel betrayed by them. The closest he'd come was a cheating girlfriend in high school who'd hooked up with one of his friends at a party. But that was quite a bit different. For starters, he got retribution not long after. And perhaps, if everything worked out, Crum would get his.

Wandering the halls, Crum found the security closet. Pressing his thumb against the glass window, the light flashed green and he heard a click inside the door. Opening it, he stepped in to find two guards watching the numerous screens.

They glanced back but didn't say anything.

Crum quickly scanned the screens, seeing five of them blank, the box completely black with a time stamp in the bottom right corner. "What's wrong with those?" He pointed at three adjoined boxes, and the two in a different area.

"No clue. They've been doing that a lot lately. Boss had em all checked out earlier, but said everything was working the way it's supposed to. They'll come back on in a few minutes." Glancing at the bottom two screens, the guard continued. "Those two are in here. And the one's up there are the main room near the kitchen."

"Guess if we're gonna do anything bad, now's the time. Smoke em if you got em, boys!" The other guard joked, silently testing their new boss.

"Have either of you seen Damion?"

"Yeah. He went into his office about three hours ago. Haven't seen him come out."

"Thank you." Without another word, Crum made his way out into the hall and turned right. Navigating the corridors, he watched for any signs of the elvish writing hidden throughout the complex. He wouldn't be able to get into Damion's office through the main door. But if he could find the tunnels, maybe he could get that other way.

Approaching a set of double doors, Crum froze, realizing where he was. He knew the cameras couldn't see him. The net made both him and Ray invisible to them. But he needed to make sure no guards were around. And if he continued through the next doors, he'd find two of them. Why they guarded the basement entrance, he couldn't answer. But who was he to argue with the post? Perhaps if there was a sewer entrance, someone could sneak in. But that seemed a little too farfetched. Who in their right mind would sneak into a dinner party through a sewer entrance? This wasn't the movies.

Bringing himself back to the now, Crum blurred his vision and carefully searched the floors and walls for the hidden writing. Elves were funny that way. They were naturally good at finding what was hidden, so they always hid their art and writing in a similar fashion to prevent non-elves from discovering it. Sure enough, a strange dark brown sigil appeared in the polished floor, near the wall. It jumped out like a stereogram coming into focus. Completing the symbols in his mind, he read the message to himself.

I make the day, born bright and retired full. But my appetite is short lived. You see me in all my glory, but I change frequently. I'm synodic, and ever revolving.

Crum recognized instantly, it was a riddle. Searching the wall, he saw a painted over box, hidden from view. Carefully, he pried against the square, feeling it move. It slid upward, revealing a dial much like the one he'd seen the previous evening. Inspecting the symbols, he noticed a trend. There were three bands, each one independent of the others. This was a combination lock. And it seemed the key was in this riddle. Silently repeating it to himself, he spun the rings, inspecting his options.

I make the day, born bright and retired full. That didn't make any sense. The options appeared to be numbers. But the face of the dial held religious symbols. Recalling the little he remembered about elven religion, Crum knew they used astronomy as symbols for their gods. Suddenly, the answer hit him. Crum pressed the symbol for Selene. The elves worshiped her in the presence of the moon. The dial face locked in, but the door didn't open. Reciting the next passage, he looked at each numbered option. *My appetite is short lived.* A full moon only lasted three days, he thought to himself, seeing three as an option. Setting the ring to align with the locked lunar face, Crum continued.

In moments, he had all three rings aligned, the combination set at three, eight, thirty. The locked face popped out, displaying a rod on the back side of it. Crum pressed the face, rod and all into the dial and a door sprang open. Quickly, he stepped inside and closed the passage.

As before, the hall was plain and uninviting. Every detail was bland and identical, save for the markings he knew to look for. Reading them as he passed, it took no time to find the crossway and elevator. Now that he'd had time to study it a bit, he was fairly certain this was once an elven safehouse, and most likely still was, without human knowledge. There were numerous suggestions that the complex had several more subterranean layers, each one accessible only by the eternal children, as the words read. Pressing the modernized button beside the elevator door, Crum waited for it to open. He could hear the pulleys behind the door moving, as the sealed cage positioned itself. The door opened and Crum stepped inside. Selecting his destination, wondering if the elevator was capable of reaching the lower layers, it ascended, carrying him toward the club owner's office.

Coming to a stop, the single door slid to the side, revealing the back side of the bookcase. A small lever, roughly four inches in length was attached to the wall just outside the elevator. Crum pulled it and the case folded out and opened for him. There, at the desk, sprawled out in a brown leather-bound chair was Damion.

He was limp, slumped where his body lay. A pile of vomit rested on the floor beside him, evidence of it on his face.

Crum rushed to the man's side, checking for a pulse. It was faint, but present. "Damion, can you hear me?"

The man's eyes slowly opened, bloodshot and searching. "Huh?" His speech was indecipherable and his mouth was slack, refusing to move.

Crum inspected the pile, noticing several partially digested pills. "Damion, what'd you take?" The orc shook the man, trying to get him to focus. Searching the desk, and floor around it, Crum found his query. Lying on its side, caked in vomit, was an orange pill bottle with a white lid. A partial bottle of rum lay not far from it in a moist stain on the carpet. "How many did you take?" Crum asked, snatching up the prescription bottle and reading the label. There were thirty pills to this prescription, and at least eight were lying on the floor.

"Ay tok o any ut ay thrrew dem ut. Sooo ay tuk da west." His head bobbed forward and back, as if trying to focus. His brown eyes worked independently of each other, the pupils shifting and resizing. They were glazed and turning yellow.

"I'm sorry about this, but it's for your own good." Crum forced his thick fingers into the man's mouth, jamming his knuckle into the hinge of his jaw. That was the only way to ensure he didn't get bitten. Probing the back of Damion's throat, he triggered his gag reflex.

Damion convulsed and hacked, his body reacting on instinct.

Ensuring it took, Crum kept his finger positioned, but to the side, granting the vomit an escape. He didn't want to drown the man after all. As soon as he felt the chunky bile, Crum jerked Damion forward and to the side, allowing him to spill out onto the already soiled floor. He counted another thirteen pills added to the mess. Confident the man was done, Crum laid him against the backrest and released him. Pressing the button on this earbud, he spoke. "Call an ambulance immediately, and send Ray to Damion's office. We're closing early tonight!"

"On it, boss." One of the guards replied.

Returning his attention to Damion, Crum walked toward the small bar and grabbed a scotch glass. Filling it with tap water, he returned to the man's side and poured just enough to help wash away the taste of stomach acid. He didn't want to give him too much in the event more pills were still in there. Last thing he wanted to do was help them activate any quicker. Setting the glass on the desk, Crum stared intently at the helpless human. "You're a stupid man, do you know that? Trying to make a permanent solution to a temporary problem. I won't tell you you're being selfish or any of that nonsense. But you're certainly stupid. Your sister is safe. She was parked at the beach with a boy."

Patrons funneled out the doors, clearly unhappy about the shortness of their evening. There had been an uproar when Ray made the announcement, but it quickly settled when he promised complete refunds. They were content with that considering the meal portion was already over and Joe, the musician of the evening, was halfway through his set.

Ray turned to the bearded man, seeing him approach. "My apologies for cutting it short. I fear it was unavoidable."

"No worries. When ambulances arrive, it's a pretty good indicator that things have become complicated. I was just happy to be here. And of course, the pay was nice." Joe smiled, taking a long draw off his vapor unit and blowing it overhead in a thick cloud.

"Let me know if you want to come back here someday. I'll see what I can do."

"Thank you. I'm sure I can make room for that, though it'll have to be a few months. I'm headed to New York in the morning."

"Understood. I'll make sure Rachel—" Ray smiled, having remembered the girl's name. "—keeps an open invitation for you. Anyway, I need to head upstairs and see what we're dealing with."

"Understood. Have a great one." Joe shook his hand and headed toward the side doors.

Turning toward the glass elevator, Ray quickly made his way inside and ascended to the upper level. Stepping into the private lounge, he noticed the office door remained open. Damion was strapped to a plastic stretcher and two paramedics tended to his needs.

Making his way into the side room, careful to stay out of their way, Ray found Crum standing near the desk. The orc's attention seemed preoccupied with the sleek device in his hands. Ray approached. "How's everything up here?" Stealing a glanced at Damion, he seemed more cognitive than before.

"They think he'll be fine. He seems to have thrown up most of the pills. They're going to keep him overnight just to be sure."

As if the statement was their cue, the paramedics rolled the gurney through the door and toward the elevator, leaving Ray and Crum to their solitude.

"I got Damion's phone but I'm having trouble operating the damn thing. Damion said Vincent's number was saved under 'VM'. But I can't get it to do anything other than tell me the time and date. It'll pop up for a moment and then go back to a black screen."

"Let me see it." Ray extended his hand, accepting the smart phone. Looking it over closely, he identified the side buttons. Pressing the one on top, the screen came alive, displaying the lock icon. Ray slid his finger across, seeing a loading icon appear. It went back to the black screen. "Damn it!"

"What?" Crum asked, confused.

"It's got a fingerprint lock. I should have known, considering all the other locks he has around here. Do you have a piece of gum?"

"Um, yeah?" Crum reached into his jacket pocket and pulled out a folding box. Handing a piece to Ray, he closed the box and stuck it back in his pocket.

Laying the phone on the desk top, Ray removed the paper and tossed the stick in his mouth, chewing vigorously. "I'll be right back."

"Um, okay?" Crum watched him bolt for the door. He was gone in the blink of an eye.

Ray pressed the button on the elevator and waited impatiently for it to open. Hearing the ding, he stepped inside and rushed toward the glass. He could see the paramedics getting ever closer to the exit. He had to catch them before they left. It seemed to take forever to start moving. Finally, reaching ground level, the only other floor this elevator traveled to, the doors opened. Ray circled the lobby and ran into the main hall just as the paramedics disappeared from sight. Charging after them, he removed the gum wad from his mouth and concealed it in his hand. He busted through the exterior doors. "Wait! We need the security code to lock up!"

The paramedics stopped, surprised by the sudden outburst.

Ray approached Damion. Gently, discretely grabbing his hand, he firmly pressed the pliable gum against the pad of his right thumb. "Damion, are you yourself enough to tell me the security code?"

The distant club owner stared blankly at Ray, seeming unable to determine who he was. Finally, he spoke, though it sounded as if his mouth was numb. "Das ecey. Co ish, Cort-knee." Damion paused, thinking through what he'd just said. "Yah, das rite. Courney."

"Courtney, like your sister's name?" Ray confirmed, removing the gum mold, and carefully hiding it in his grip in hopes it wouldn't be damaged.

"Yeah. Coretnee."

"Okay. Thank you. Get some rest." Ray took a step back, allowing the paramedics the load him into the ambulance.

Returning to the office, Crum remained where he had been, patiently awaiting Ray's return. Without a word, Ray laid the gum mold on the desk, inspecting the firm and even print he'd lifted. Opening the desk drawers, he searched for anything he could use. Finding a bottle of superglue, he set it on the glass top and grabbed a few pieces of paper.

"What are you doing?" Crum asked, watching the detective suspiciously.

"I saw this on YouTube." Ray arranged everything atop the paper so he wouldn't ruin the glass. Filling the gum mold with super glue, he poured the excess onto the paper, leaving a thin layer to settle in the print. Glancing around the room, he spotted an old coffee pot resting on the side of the minibar. Removing the pot, he made sure it was empty and turned it on. Placing the paper on the heating pad, he positioned the mold in the center. "And now we wait." Ray pulled a cigarette and fired up, waiting for the glue to dry.

It took no time at all for the liquid to solidify and turn hard. Ray removed the gum mold from the paper and separated it from the hardened glue. It took some time to get it apart, but when he was finished he had a perfect replica of Damion's thumbprint. Pressing the print to the phone and awakening it, the scan took and the screen came to life.

"That seems like a major breech in security." Crum said, watching in astonishment. "What if that phone belonged to some government agent and had all sorts of state secrets on it?"

"Then I guess they'd be better off using an encrypted pass code. I learned a long time ago that if someone wants in bad enough, they're going to find a way. Locks only keep honest people out. But honest people don't typically try to get into places they don't belong in the first place." Scrolling through the contacts, Ray found the number saved to *VM*. Clicking it, he selected the text icon and wrote a brief message. That seemed the best way to disguise who was actually sending the message. If he called, Vincent would know the voice wasn't Damion's. And there was no reason why Ray would be calling from Damion's phone. Rereading the message, he showed it to Crum, in case the brute had any suggestions before he hit send.

I wanted to inform you that Ray has gone over your head. A meeting has been arranged with Dominic DeMarco, through means of Kevin Agnello. I hope this helps make things right between us. Here's his number if you want to contact him.

Crum read the text a second time. "Looks good to me. Though what are you going to do if he checks with this Kevin guy?"

"He won't. He'll see it as a challenge and come for me directly. DeMarco's underbosses have a working relationship and little else. They tend to take it personally when one steps on the other's toes." With no further input, Ray sent the message, watching it deliver.

A few minutes later, the phone dinged and a message displayed.

Thank you for the heads up. I'll look into it. Send the number again. It didn't show up in the first message.

"That's our cue." Ray quickly typed in the traceable number he'd been provided for such purposes and hit send. He purposely didn't send it the first time. He wanted to make sure Vincent would play ball first. A minute later, his phone rang. Quickly answering it, he heard heavy breathing on the other end. "Hello?"

"This is Vincent Merlot."

"How'd you get my number?" Ray asked, indignantly.

"I have my resources. Listen, I heard you've made a deal with Kevin Agnello to meet with DeMarco. I don't like being crossed like that. When you make a deal with me, you stick to it. Do we understand each other?"

"The only thing I understand is I made a deal with you that you didn't honor. Then you ice some dude in a vain attempt to flip it on my boy. I don't like the way you do business. It's nothing personal. Kevin can at least make things happen for me.

You don't like it, take it up with him." Ray remained quiet for a moment, letting the sloppy gangster contemplate his options.

"I think we need to discuss this face to face. Be at the Loews Hotel on South Beach in twenty minutes." Vincent hung up before Ray could argue the point.

Smiling, Ray tucked his phone away. "We're on. He wants to meet us in twenty minutes."

"You know he's going to take this as a personal insult, don't you?" Crum asked, hoping the human realized the danger he'd placed himself in.

"Yeah. But what options do we have? I'll call Anderson on the way and have him track my phone. Hopefully we can hold out until backup arrives."

The Pandora Gambit

Levi Samuel

Chapter 12
Battle Buddies

The metallic red Maserati raced across Venetian Way toward Miami Beach. The engine purred, seeming to enjoy the higher speeds. Shooting around the lower levels of traffic at the hour, Ray glanced at an illuminated sign towering over what appeared to be a bank on one of the islands. It was already 11:17. He had three minutes to reach Loews Hotel.

Leaving the edge of Rivo Alto Island, Ray glanced over the water, stretching along both sides of the long bridge. The lights of a rather large yacht were rapidly approaching, and the raising indicators of the drawbridge began to flash. He didn't have time to wait for it. Mashing the accelerator pedal, the car lunged forward, proudly displaying it had plenty of power to go.

In no time at all, they crossed Belle Isle, another section of bridge, and found themselves back on land. 17th Street loomed just ahead. Slinging around the mild curve where the road became Dade Boulevard, Ray veered right to stay on 17th. Here the traffic increased but was far from rush hour levels. Speeding along the blacktop, they passed numerous buildings and intersections, riddled along the large island. Cutting a right onto Collins Avenue, the tires gripped refusing to let out the slightest squeal. Guided by intuition, Ray corrected and the car straightened. Mashing the peddle, they flew toward their destination. On the left, the large hotel could be seen. Ray slowed and turned onto the circle drive, labeled 16th.

The drive was covered by numerous palm trees, nearly blocking out the night sky. Pulling into one of the few remaining parking spots, Ray turned off the ignition and climbed out of the car.

Following suit, Crum emerged, running his fingers through his short, black hair in hopes of settling it from the windy drive. "What do you expect?" He asked, knowing the human was wondering the same thing.

"I don't know. It's unlikely he'll try anything here. Too much of a scene. But I also doubt he'll put us in touch with DeMarco unless he has no choice. We have to remember, we're dealing with a snake. Nothing more. If we're careful, we can handle him without getting bitten. But caution is needed."

"He seems more like a thug to me." Crum stated earnestly.

"That too, albeit a high ranking one. He'll do whatever it takes to keep his power. And since we've challenged that, he's going to want to make a point." Ray approached the hotel lobby. Seeing a couple making their way from the glass doors, he silenced himself. There was no sense in providing unneeded commentary to those who didn't need to hear it.

A brand new stretched Cadillac Escalade rested in front of the entrance. Its flawless white paint job seemed to glow in the night. The driver stood near the center, facing the lobby doors, hands folded one over the other in front of him. With trained precision, his body never moved, but his voice carried, reaching only those meant to hear it. "Mister Bradley, Mister Crumble?"

The pair paused, realizing now the man was staring at them. "This way, please." He moved in perfect precision, nearly robotic in nature, but extremely fluid. His pale skin stood in stark contrast to the midnight black suit clothing him. Every detail of his visage announced him as the chauffeur he was. Reaching the rear door, he opened it and extended a hand, inviting them in.

"And so it begins." Ray stated absently, climbing into the spacious vehicle.

Crum followed, ensuring his pistol was tucked safely in his waist. He didn't enjoy using it, but under such circumstances he was glad to have it.

The door closed behind them, bringing the wonders of the private limousine to life. Subtle lighting trimmed every contour of the ceiling and floor. A plush bench ran the length on one side of the compartment, and another smaller, one lined the back, where Ray and Crum sat. A mini bar rested along the wall opposite the long bench, and an expansive entertainment center was mounted above it, complete with various digitally displayed buttons, controls, and knobs.

Ray noticed a similar console was mounted above his head, allowing one to use it without getting up.

At the far end of the compartment, a man sat facing them. He looked familiar, but neither Ray nor Crum could place where they'd seen him before.

At that moment, the limo started to move. One of the screens flickered to life, and a map appeared, detailing their exact location.

Ray glanced out the window beside him, checking to see if the map was accurate. Surely, it was, but he wanted to be sure. To his surprise, he couldn't see through the tinted glass.

"I assure you, it's accurate." The man stated blankly, his voice carrying a heavy accent that triggered where they'd seen him. Although it wasn't him they'd seen, but his brother.

"Yuri?" Crum questioned, scooting closer to get a better look. "How can this be?"

"No. I'm not Yuri. My name is Viktor. Yuri was my twin."

"So, Vincent gave you the chance to kill the men responsible for your brother's death? How generous of him." Ray stated coldly, internally preparing himself. He needed to be ready for the moment when he'd have to draw and shoot.

"No! Vincent doesn't know I'm here. He plan to have you killed, yes. But not my job. I'm not stupid. I hear rumors. I know Vincent kill my brother and try to blame it on you. This why I'm here." Viktor replied, reaching for a small box resting beside him.

It was wrapped in red foil and had silver lace tied into a bow at the top, reminding Ray of a Christmas present. "I have map turned on so you know where you go. This also for you." He handed the wrapped present to Ray and leaned back against the white leather of his seat.

"Why are you doing this? If you're not here to kill us, why do you care?" Ray asked, taking the box.

"You don't remember me, do you?" Viktor paused, allowing a moment of reflection. With no response, he continued. "Afghanistan, March '08. I was in convoy headed back to Bagram. Mission was over and my unit headed home. IED explode beside us, flipping truck. I don't remember how long I there, but only had twelve bullets left between three guys. Next morning, I hear gun shots. But not hitting us anymore. One of my battle brothers bled out in the night. The other shot himself. I only survivor when unit find us. I remember. Man pick me up and carry me to medic. Month later I on a plane going home."

Ray closed his eyes, recalling the events as if they were happening before him.

"That man was you." The Russian continued. "When I came home, I had nothing. No clothes. No food. No home. My brother, Yuri was working for man called, Carmine. He tell me about good money doing easy job. Not long after, Vincent took his place and been trouble ever since. Vincent kill my brother. You my brother now, as much as when we in sand together. This why I'm here. I can't take Vincent myself. Nobody support me. But you can. He try to kill you. If you kill him first. Nobody retaliate. I promise you that."

Pulling the silver string, Ray opened the box. Inside rested an olive colored ball about the size of a plum. It had a lever and a pin protruding from the top. And in black, stamped on the green housing said, *M67.* "You expect me to kill him with a grenade?" Ray asked, both stunned and surprised.

"I apologize it not much. You have gun I assume. Doesn't matter how you do it. Vincent not stop coming for you until you dead, or he dead. I prefer him." Glancing at the screen displaying their blip on the map, Viktor continued. "Look like he taking you to shipyard. If you need help, now the time to call for it. We be there in four minutes."

Glancing at Crum, the orc offered nothing but a nod. That was enough. If Crum believed the man, he could too. They were in this together. Pulling his phone, Ray dialed the number, hearing the captain's voice on the other end. "Sir, an update to our earlier conversation. We're in a white limo, Escalade, headed to the shipyard off 5th and Miami Avenue." Ray paused, waiting for an opening to continue. "Yes, Sir. On the river. We have a couple minutes before we arrive. An informant risked himself to let us know it's an execution when we get there." Glancing at the map, he saw they were approaching the bridge overlooking the yard. "Yes, Sir. I've got to go. Try to hurry." Tucking his phone away, he returned his attention to Viktor. "What now?"

"Now we wait. Good luck. I wish I could offer more."

"You've helped more than you know." Ray offered, removing the grenade from the box.

The limo turned onto a side street and went around the block to reconnect to 5th. Pulling into the shipyard, Ray didn't have to see it to know they were passing through the gates. The texture of the road changed. It was now bumpy, like that of a dirt road, rather than the smooth paved feel of the street. The Escalade came to a stop, sitting idle in the middle of the yard.

"So this is it, huh?" Ray asked absently, speaking to himself as much as his companions.

"It is. Be careful and good luck." Without hesitation, Viktor reached into the gap between the seat cushions and drew a black pistol. A suppressor had been fixed to the end of the muzzle.

Bringing it around, he placed it to his temple and pulled the trigger.

"No!" Ray shouted, one hand on his own firearm, the other reaching for the man across from him. It was too late. A mild pop echoed, and a spray of red exploded against the interior wall and ceiling. Realizing there was nothing he could do, Ray collapsed, his knees impacting the carpeted floor. Eyes closed, he took a deep breath and exhaled. Sniffing, a sense of composure returned and he brought himself back up. Turning to Crum, he drew his own pistol and removed the clip, ensuring it was loaded to capacity. Checking the chambered round, he reinstalled the clip. "Are you ready?"

Crum removed his own gun, ensuring it was ready to go. "As ready as I can be. Don't take what happened here personally. He was hurt and looking for a way out. Neither of us saw it coming."

Ray nodded his agreement, unable to give it voice. Tucking his Colt back into its holster, he picked the grenade off the floor and reached for the chromed door handle. The night sky peeked through a narrow crack in the seal. Ray pushed the door open and stepped out, Crum on his flank.

Outside, a black Lincoln Navigator rested about twenty feet from them. It sat idle, displaying the passenger's side profile. The windows were closed, their tinted surface locking out any clue as to who was inside. The only signs of life were the beaming headlights, illuminating a pile of salvaged metal that had been roughly stacked beside an old decommissioned ship, and the red glow from the taillights catching the rolling exhaust fumes.

Only now did Ray realize how cold the night was growing. He hadn't felt it thirty minutes earlier, cruising with the top down. But now, after everything that had happened in that short amount of time, he felt a chill in the air, as if death lingered to claim him. Listening to the door behind him close, the limo started to pull away. He could hear the rocks crunch beneath the tires as it distanced itself, removing any chance for cover he and Crum might have had.

The rear door of the Navigator opened just enough to allow the portly gangster to step out. Both Ray and Crum could tell someone else was inside, but they weren't able to see who.

No sooner than Vincent was clear, he closed the door and took position where he stood. His pen-striped suit caught the moonlight, detailing the numerous faint lines running its length. The crisp folds at the front of his pants were crumpled slightly from sitting too long. His spectator wingtip shoes were already collecting dust from the compact dirt he was standing upon. And his bulging belly threatened the single clasped button of his jacket. But the most unsettling thing about his appearance, was the cherry glow of his cigar. There was something about that red-orange glowing ember that suggested he was comfortable with the atrocities he'd come here to commit. "You've been a thorn in my side since the moment I met you. I can't say you'll be missed, or even remembered for that matter." Blowing a thick cloud of smoke, Vincent took a step to the side, ensuring he was clear.

Both the front and rear side windows of the Navigator lowered. Three men could be seen inside the vehicle. Two up front, one of the them the driver, and one in back. The two closest to the windows lifted flat-black, metallic instruments and pointed them at the two, unprotected men.

Glancing from the machine guns to Crum, and back again, Ray felt as if the world was moving in slow motion. "MAC-10s!" He shouted, searching for cover. Several pops echoed all around him and dust flew from where the numerous bullets hit. There was no doubt in his mind that both he and Crum would be beyond lucky if either of them got out of this at all, let alone unscathed. He wanted to return fire, but there was no time. He needed to find cover. A sharp pain erupted in his body. He knew instantly he'd been hit. He just didn't know where.

Reacting on instinct, Crum twisted and grabbed his human counterpart. Muscles bulging, the orc lifted Ray and threw him toward a pile of refuse. It wasn't perfect cover, but it was better than nothing.

Ray crashed into a stack of steel drums. They tumbled down around him, covering him in bits of flaked paint and rust from years of disuse. The detective worked to dig his way from the collapsed stack, realizing Crum was still in the open.

Seeing Ray safe, as safe as he could be, Crum grabbed a steel beam lying in the dirt just ahead of him. He didn't know what it was, but he could see the welds where it was attached to a large plate that had been caked with dirt and mud. Prying it up with all his strength, it separated from the ground, forming a makeshift wall. Bullets plinked off the steel barrier, denting it with each shot. Weighing his options, Crum lifted the iron device and carried it toward Ray, hoping it would continue to hold against the rapid fire of machine guns.

Digging his way free of the drums, Ray peeked over the pile of metal. A barrage of bullets riddled the area, but it was clear they didn't know exactly where he was. Seeing Crum, cowering behind what appeared to be a makeshift shield, Ray drew his gun and took aim at the SUV. In an attempt to calm himself, he exhaled and squeezed the trigger. His bullet hit the post between the front and back seats. He was still shaken. His body trembled. He needed to breathe. Only then would he be able to hit his target.

Hearing the machine guns slow, Crum knew at least one of them was reloading. This was his chance. Setting the bottom edge of his wall in the dirt, he drew his Desert Eagle. Leaning around the barrier, Crum popped off four shots. He ducked back, just as another volley riddled his position. Something caught his eye as he returned to cover. The grenade Ray had been given was lying in the dirt. It seemed the young human had dropped it when he'd been thrown. Counting the shots as best he could, Crum braced the wall and scurried out as low as possible. Wrapping his hand around the drab colored device, he pulled himself back, feeling the dirt explode around him. Removing the safety clip, Crum squeezed the spoon and pulled the pin. Releasing the lever, he cooked it off. "One-thousand-one. One-thousand-two." Flinging the grenade over the shield, he waited, bracing himself tightly against the makeshift barrier.

Ray noticed the grenade hit the ground and roll under the SUV. Crum was way too close to it. Before he could shout, it exploded. Ray took cover, hearing a secondary blast. He knew the fuel tank had ignited. Popping up from his cover, Ray surveyed the scene.

Both Crum, and the wall he'd been using were nowhere to be seen. Vincent was lying on the ground, crawling away from the enflamed Navigator. And the men inside were bruised and bloodied, but the two in the front appeared to still be alive. He couldn't say the same for the one in back. Taking aim, Ray cautiously approached the vehicle.

The man in the front passenger's seat saw him. Weakly, he raised the machine gun, trying to turn it on the man.

"Don't do it!" Ray shouted, his gun aimed and ready to fire. Part of him wished the man would listen. But it was clear he wasn't going to. The barrel reached the threshold of the shattered window and Ray pulled the trigger, putting three rounds in the man's chest. He fell still. Ray limped closer to the destroyed vehicle. Reaching through the shattered window, he removed the gun from the man's possession. Now that he'd had a moment, he could tell the pain was in his leg. Glancing down, dirt and red liquid stained his pants. He wasn't sure how bad it was, but he didn't have time to worry about it yet. He was still mobile, that was all that mattered. Working his way around, Ray pistol whipped the driver and laid his head against the steering wheel.

He had to be certain the man wouldn't go for a weapon. And without handcuffs, unconscious was the next best option. He preferred to remove him from the burning vehicle, but it seemed most of the damage had already been done. He was at little risk were he sat.

Crum opened his eyes. He was sore, but he'd live. Trying to move, he felt as if every muscle in his body screamed in protest. It was dark. But not night time dark. He'd expected that. This was enclosed space dark. Straining against his confines, Crum felt them shift. He flexed his arms and shoved as hard as he could. The barrier he'd been using covered him completely. Pushing it from him, he was now able to see what had happened. The explosion had blasted him back and he'd been buried in a pile of twisted and jagged metal. His side was scraped pretty bad, but nothing had pierced him, which was good considering the condition of it all. He'd likely die from tetanus if it had. Groaning, Crum pulled himself from the pile and searched the area for Ray. He could hear sirens in the distance. Red and blue lights flashed on the surrounding buildings. Help was on the way.

Having secured the vehicle and ensured all firearms were accounted for, Ray stumbled over to Vincent, who'd crawled toward the edge of the dirt lot. His legs were shredded, several pieces of debris protruding from his lower half. It wouldn't surprise Ray one bit if he never walked again. His aim trained on the wounded criminal, Ray took position over him. "It's over Vincent. You've lost."

"Kill me then and be done with it!" Vincent spat, anger in his voice.

"I'll do you one better. Vincent Merlot, you're under arrest for the murder of Yuri Sokolov, the attempted murder of a police officer, conspiracy to commit criminal activity, distribution of narcotics, and quite frankly, for pissing me off!"

Chapter 13
The Chase

A steady beep pulsed from the computer screen mounted beside the hospital bed. Heartrate was steady, and vitals read good.

Ray stood over the man, strapped to the cot, unable to move more than his head.

Vincent began to stir, searching the world around him. His lip curled in hatred at the sight of the man above him. It didn't take long to realize he was trapped, unable to do anything. Both his arms were wrapped in padded straps, as was his torso. Glancing down, both legs were capped and bandaged. The normally white gauze was stained brown and yellow where his legs had been amputated. The reality of it all came crashing in around him. "What do you want?" His voice was full of venom.

"The same thing I wanted before you complicated all of this. A meeting with DeMarco." Ray answered simply.

"And why would I give it to you? You know as well as I, I'm a dead man if I give him up. Besides, it's not like I can personally introduce you anymore."

"It's more a matter of self-preservation. You're already a dead man. It depends on you how soon that death is."

"What do you mean?" Vincent asked, feeling another shot of morphine rush through his body. It began in his left arm, a burning heat that traveled from the needle and toward his heart. From there, it went everywhere. He relaxed against the pillow, as if all his strength had been robbed.

"You're going away for a very long time whether you help us or not. Either way, DeMarco is going to learn about you. If you go into the system and we don't get him, how long do you think you'll last? But if you help us, I can ensure you go away someplace DeMarco will never find you. It's up to you. Your life is finished either way." Ray claimed calmly, feeling no remorse for the man's position.

"Has news of our encounter hit the press yet?"

"Not yet. We've made certain to keep it quiet. You're no good to us if he thinks you've been compromised."

"Alright. I'll set it up. But I want to be someplace he'll never think to look for me."

"That'll be no problem. I'll return in a few hours with a plea bargain. You can make the call after it's been signed." Refusing the give the man time to change his mind, Ray turned and marched from the private room.

Crum sat in a chair outside. He was sore, but he'd live. The scratches along his side were already beginning to heal. He just had to be sure they didn't get infected. Seeing Ray exit the room, he stood and waited for him to approach. "Did he agree?"

"Yes. Though I think you'll need to call your people to house him. I had to promise he'd be put someplace were DeMarco will never find him."

"No worries. How's the leg?" Crum asked, noticing Ray's limp.

"I'll be all right. Doc said it was little more than a flesh wound. Bullet mostly hit the meat." Pausing for a moment, as if to find his thoughts, Ray continued. "I need to speak with Anderson and have a plea deal written up. I figure that's the only way to lock Vincent into his promise."

Sunlight beamed across Biscayne Bay, as it did every day. But today was a little different. Today was a day of success. And nobody was going to get in the way of that.

Ray slammed on the brakes, honking his horn at the guy in front of him.

The man threw his arms up, staring through his gold tinted glasses. The baggy shorts around his legs displayed much of his underpants, and he wore a gold chain with no shirt. "What?" He asked indignantly, as if he hadn't just stepped in front of a moving car.

"Get out of the road!" Ray shouted, shaking his head in disgust. "Damn idiots! They act as if they own the road."

Crum chuckled to himself, seeing the man's frustration when moments before he'd been joyous and good tempered. "You tell him." Crum added, urging the human on.

Sighing his annoyance, Ray accelerated slightly and pulled into the lot. Vincent had come through for them, not that he'd had much choice. They wanted as little choice as possible when arranging this deal. Nosing into the first open stall, Ray turned off the car and climbed out. Despite the minor annoyance of jaywalkers, he was having a great day. He was wearing his favorite suit, white with a red silk liner. And the judge who'd signed off on the plea bargain was entirely on board with their plan.

"I think I'm going to do a quick perimeter before I head in. I'd like to get a feel for what we're walking into."

"Suit yourself. I'm gonna go get acquainted with DeMarco. I'll save you a seat." Tossing the keys into the air, Ray caught them and strutted toward the small tiki bar overlooking the bay. He hadn't reached the main doors when he noticed the heavy security lingering about. This had to be the place. And provided Vincent hadn't anticipated his own capture, there was no way he could have tipped off DeMarco. Ray had listened to the conversation himself.

Making his way past the numerous muscle, and into the fairly open main room, Ray noticed something else out of the ordinary.

At least out of the ordinary to his new reality. There were a substantial number of elves here. A larger population than any other he'd seen. In this room alone, there were four, and at least two more outside. He made a mental note to keep track of them, but not so much as to draw attention to himself. He approached the bay side doors, being stopped by two of the guards. Both wore dark suits and sunglasses, despite standing under the cabana. "I'm here to see Dominic DeMarco." Ray counted four tables resting on the open patio.

Three had been moved near the outer edge, and the last sat dead center. A man wearing a white suit sat in one of the basket weaved chairs, his back to the door. The man's hand slowly raised, and the guards stepped aside, despite having never looked his direction.

Marching between them, Ray approached the central table. It was a nice day, and there were many people on this private section of beach. That wasn't uncommon, Ray just found it strange. The larger, public beaches were on the other side of the island. Doing a quick head count, there were seven guards out here, each one keeping distance. Some were meant to look like civilians, and while they did a near perfect job, it was their eyes that gave them away. They kept scanning the area, as if searching for something. "Dominic DeMarco, I presume?" Ray asked, extending a hand to the seated man. Only now did he realize this man was an elf. His long, brown hair draped carelessly about his shoulders, though it seemed to fall perfectly in every way.

Dominic stood and shook the man's hand. "You presume correctly. Please, take a seat, Mister Bradley." The elf waited for him to obey before returning to his own chair.

Ray felt compelled to comply. He couldn't explain it. Sure, he was going to sit anyway, but there was something about the elf's voice that made him feel as if he had no choice in the matter. "Don't mind if I do." Ray took the seat to Dominic's left, selected for the sole purpose that it didn't block Dominic's view of the bay. There was a deep compulsion within that screamed the horrors he'd face if he sat anywhere else. "So, Mister DeMarco. I assume you've been told why I wished to meet with you?"

"Of course. You don't wish to work with Vincent. I can't say I'm surprised. I find him quite abrasive myself. Though from a business standpoint, we can't always select who we wish to work with. On occasion one must bite the bullet, so to speak. Though I'm pleased to say I do not believe this to be one of those times. Would you, Mister Bradley?"

Ray was lost in the complexity of the words. He was hearing two conversations at once. One came from the elf's mouth. The other, his own mind. And both layered atop one another, creating a deep confusion. "I'm sorry, what was the question?"

Dominic smiled and leaned forward, lifting a tiki glass from the table. The liquid was an orange color and had several chunks of pineapple and cherries floating inside, complete with a tiny umbrella. Taking a sip, he rephrased. "Are you happy for the chance to work together?"

"Why wouldn't I be? You've already proven yourself a much greater host than the aforementioned Mister Merlot."

The elf smiled a wicked smile and sat his glass on the table. "Excellent. So, I want you to do something for me. Perhaps afterward, we can get down to business."

"Anything you need. You have but to name it." Ray declared, lost in the elf's piercing gaze.

"I want you to walk toward the bay. Once you reach the water, keep walking. When it swallows you whole, keep walking. Only after your lungs have exploded inside your chest are you to stop. Will you do that for me? I wish to send a message to the Miami Police Department."

Ray couldn't tell if the words came from the elf's mouth or his head. It could have been both for all he knew. "Sure, Mister

DeMarco. I can do that for you." Ray stood and turned toward the Bay. It wouldn't be a long walk by any means.

"Ray, that's Wright!" Crum jumped over the small banister around the patio, drawing his gun.

Startled by the sudden commotion, Ray shook himself, trying to get the impulse out of his head. What the hell had the elf done to him? Seeing Crum, he glanced around, unsure what was happening.

"Ray! He's getting away!" Crum shouted, laying cover fire toward two of the guards who'd drawn weapons.

Ray saw the elf jump the banister. He was running through the sand, toward a small dock. The gunshots roused him. Turning, Ray saw Crum charge after the elf. He leapt the railing with ease and nearly fell in the sand.

Catching himself, Crum ran as fast and as hard as he could. He had to catch Wright before he got away.

Ray watched, dumbfounded. It seemed odd, watching an orc chase an elf across the beach. But stranger things had happened—What was he thinking? No, they hadn't. This was the strangest thing he'd ever seen, and he was simply letting it happen before his own eyes. He needed to do something.

Wright climbed the side of the dock, scaling the chain linked gate blocking the ramp. Running to the end of the wood and rubber protrusion, he jumped onto a blue and white cigarette boat, kicking its owner off the side. The man hit the water with a splash. Turning the key, still in the ignition, Wright fired it up and pulled the control lever into the reverse position. Rushing toward the nose, he unwrapped the mooring line and tossed it off. The boat roared and backed away from the dock.

Reaching the gated ramp, Crum had to do something quick. Wright was getting away and he had no way to follow him. But Wright had stolen a boat. Crum could do the same. Two people, Crum guessed them to be teenagers by human standard, were at the other end of the walkway, having just come in. They wore lifejackets, and their rubber body suits dripped, appearing to have been drenched at some point. But it wasn't the kids themselves he cared about. It was their toys. Each one had a large Sea-Doo jet ski, resting peaceably in the boat slip. Crum ran toward them. "Kid, I need to borrow your thing." He looked the toys up and down. The larger of the two was green and white, while the other was red and yellow. He guessed the larger one would be faster.

They laughed, clearly believing it to be a joke. They were more concerned with the guy in the water than the one before them. "Good one. Let me take another spin. Maybe I'll give you a run afterward."

"Kid, I'm not playing. You see that guy out there?" Crum pointed to the evading boat. "He's a bad man. He's hurt a lot of people. And if I don't stop him he's going to hurt even more."

"Dude, I'm eighteen. Why you talking to me like I'm a kid?"

The other boy, clearly a few years younger than the first, laughed.

"Eighteen, huh?" Crum asked, looking from the kid to the shrinking power boat, and back again.

"Yeah, what of it?"

Crum lifted the kid off the jet ski with one hand and tossed him into the water. "Are you eighteen too?" He asked the other one.

"N—No!"

"Good. When someone needs your help, you give it. Don't be a dick. Now how do I use this thing?" Crum straddled the small craft, fidgeting with the controls.

"You need one of these." The younger of the two boys held up the safety clip that had been ripped out when the first boy went flying. "And then you turn that knob and push that button. From there, you just push that lever by your thumb to go faster.

They're auto trim, so you shouldn't have to mess with that." He pointed at a rocker switch on the right-side control.

"Got it!" Crum took the safety clip from the kid and stuck it behind the kill button. Following directions, he fired it up, cranked the handlebars, and hit the lever to pull from the dock.

The guards didn't seem to care about him. Their focus was on Crum. At least the few that were shooting anyway. They were the elves. Most of the humans seemed confused, or outright scared. He didn't have time to deal with all of that. Crum was in pursuit. And he needed to provide backup. Jumping the small, wooden fence that separated the parking lot from the beach and bar house, Ray felt the pain in his leg renew. He was glad now he hadn't given chase. As quick as he could, he made his way to the car and jumped into the driver's seat. Slamming the key into the ignition, the engine purred to life, still warm from his arrival.

Ray glanced into the bay, seeing the boat Wright was on. And a little way behind it, he saw the smaller craft Crum had confiscated. He needed to get closer. Or at the very least, keep them in sight until they could surround the boat. Backing from his parking spot, Ray pulled onto Alton Road. He wasn't overly familiar with the area, and as far as he could see, there wasn't a road that ran along the beach. At least not on this part. Shifting into first, Ray popped the clutch and took off. Nearly immediately, he turned onto a side alley that ran beneath MacArthur, and corrected north onto 5th Street.

Gaining speed, buildings flew past. Ray could see his query every so often, but he desperately needed to get closer. And it was clear this wasn't doing it. Crossroads flew past, but none seemed to get him closer to the beach. 10th, 11th, 12th, 13th, each one took him further inland. Finally, he saw one that offered some advancement. Hooking Left, Ray slid around the corner onto 14th, and again, back right onto Bay Road. He was closer to the water than he'd been yet, and was gaining. But he still had a way to go before he'd be atop of Wright. Passing 14th Terrace, a large building came into sight, obstructing his vision. It had to have been at least three blocks long. Ray saw a large sign that said, Flamingo Tower. He wasn't sure exactly what it was, but apparently, they held some real estate.

Finally, the building ended, and Ray was able to see the ocean again. Unfortunately, neither Wright, nor Crum were anywhere in sight. Pressing the call button on his steering wheel, Ray cycled through the frequently dialed numbers, finding the one he desired on his radio display. Hitting the button again, it rang.

"Anderson!"

"Captain. This is Ray. We met DeMarco. Things got out of hand. We're in hot pursuit, Crumble by sea, me by land. He's heading toward the southern tip of Belle Isle. I need you to call the Coast Guard— Oh, shit, I've got to go, Sir!" Ray killed the call. The end of the road rapidly approached. Seeing his last chance to alter course, he turned east onto Lincoln Road, heading inland. That wasn't the direction he desired, but he had no choice. It was either that or go swimming.

Scanning his left, Ray searched for any road that would continue north. Finally, he spotted one that didn't end in the bay. Turning onto West Avenue, Ray suddenly knew where he was. Turning left again, he skidded across 17th Street, narrowly avoiding an oncoming bus. Correcting, he shifted and launched forward with blinding speed. The road curved and blended into Dade Boulevard, becoming Venetian Way just as quickly. Finally, Ray was over water, just as he'd intended. But now he had to find Crum. And preferably, Wright as well. Scanning as much as he could, while keeping an eye on the road, Ray caught a glimpse of two racing crafts in the distance. Neither were large. But that had to be them.

Ray crossed Belle Isle, watching as best he could with so much distance between them, but they were getting closer. Nearing the end of the man-made island, Ray caught sight of the blue and white boat, followed shortly by the green and white jet ski. They were much closer than he'd thought, and still gaining. It seemed all his racing around had finally paid off. But now he had to get the boat stopped.

Crossing onto the next section of bridge, Ray saw the flashing red lights of the Venetian Causeway. The boom barriers were starting to lower, which meant the bridge was raising. Stealing a glance, he saw the cause. A large sailboat was coming through and would need the space. Looking to the other side, it was apparent Wright was going to pass the bridge before the sailboat. But it was going to be close. He didn't have time to wait. Taking a deep breath, Ray made his decision. Fastening his seatbelt, he mashed the gas pedal and shot around the stalled cars, stopped at the boom. Wright was directly underneath him. Now all he had to do was something stupid.

Ray bashed through the boom arm, watching it hinge away from him. The bridge had just started to ascend when he hit. Cutting the wheel as hard as he could, the tires caught and changed direction, launching him out over the bay. "This is gonna hurt!" Ray screamed, feeling weightless, hoping he'd timed it right. A loud crash brought him to a sudden halt. Ray looked up from the deployed airbag that had cushioned his face from the steering wheel. Slowly, he glanced around, realizing where he was. The nose of his car was buried in the rear of the stolen boat.

Waves from the massive sailboat rocked him, making him feel small by comparison. People gathered on the side to see the spectacle. Shouts and waves, and camera flashes caught his attention.

"You idiot! Do you realize what you've done?"

Ray turned, seeing Wright climb over the damaged fiberglass. He had a gun in hand, and the look in his eyes said he was going to use it.

"Wright! Put it down!" Crum shouted, his gun drawn and aimed at the elf. The jet ski floated gently toward the stalled boat, bumping lightly into the side.

"You choose this human over me?" Wright sounded offended. "He's nothing. Dead in a few short years compared to you and me. And you choose him?"

"He didn't betray and leave me for dead!" Crum replied, refusing to lower his weapon.

"Left you for dead? If I wanted you dead, you'd be dead. What? Do you really think I would have done all this and not made absolutely sure you were dead if that was what I wanted? No, Crum. I wanted you alive. Now, if you're going to shoot me, I recommend you do it. Because one of us is going to die right here, right now. And it's not going to be—"

Crum pulled the trigger.

"Anything new?" Ray glanced through the one-way glass, looking into the interrogation room. Returning his attention to Crum, he felt a kinship to the large orc.

Crum's gaze was fixed upon the imprisoned elf, cuffed to the table on the other side of the glass. "No. He hasn't said a word to anyone. I feel like he's waiting for me."

"Perhaps you should talk to him then."

"And say what? I should have killed him. Or, we're being sent back to Chicago within the hour. What can I possibly say to him that he doesn't already know?" Crum eyed the bandages holding the elf's useless arm in place. The bullet had shattered the bone at the shoulder, killing the limb instantly.

"If it's any consolation, you saved my life. Which I'm eternally grateful for." Ray pleaded sincerely.

"You would have done the same for me."

A knock echoed from the door. Ray approached, twisting the knob. "Yes?"

Alice stood on the other side. Her blonde hair was pulled into her usual pony tail, and her wide brimmed glasses amplified her eyes. "I'm sorry to interrupt. Captain Anderson told me to make sure you saw this." She rushed through the door, nearly forcing Ray aside. Grabbing the antique remote atop the filing cabinet, Alice pointed it at the wood-grain patterned tube television, mounted in the corner. Quickly flipping to the correct channel, a woman appeared wearing a fuchsia pink top and black, flower-patterned pants.

"—as of yet, no one has come forward with any information about this unexplained outbreak. Reports of *Monsters* are coming in from all over the city. But this doesn't appear to be an isolated incident. Major metropolises, such as New York City, St. Louis, Chicago, Huston, Los Angeles, and many of the surrounding areas are also under attack by this strange epidemic. Hold on!" She paused a moment as if listening to a conversation unheard through the camera. "This just in. The CDC has ordered all infected areas to be quarantined immediately, until more can be learned about this outbreak."

The scene shrank to a small window in the upper right corner and a news room came into view. Two people, a middle-aged man, and a woman seemingly similar in years, sat at a large desk. The channel's logo was displayed proudly on the front side of the desk in big, red and white letters. "Be careful out there, Karen." The man said, reading from what appeared to be a script.

Alice turned off the TV and sat the remote where she'd found it. Gaze locked on Ray, she waited for any sign of concern. "The phones have been going crazy for the last hour."

"Thank you, Alice. We'll be up shortly."

Confusion on her face, she slowly turned toward Crum. Her eyes widened, and she cautiously backed away from him. "What the hell is he?"

"Alice? What are you talking about?" Ray approached her, unsure what was happening.

"She's been infected." Crum stated calmly, refusing to look away from Wright.

Wright smiled widely, clear in his victory. Certain Crum was watching, he spoke. "It's only a matter of time now. A new age of elves begins!"

"They've all been infected. I need to call headquarters." Refusing to delay a moment longer, Crum broke away from the glass and marched out the door. Things had just gotten extremely complicated and he needed direction.

Watching the large creature leave the room, Alice calmed herself. "What's going on, Ray?"

"It's a long story. But for now, we need to get you to the lab. You've been infected with Pandora and we need to see what we can do to find an antidote."

Anderson sat upright in his chair, going over the reports that had piled in front of him. Examining the pictures of the destroyed Maserati, he sighed deeply, laying them aside. Glancing at the disciplinary report, tucked neatly inside the file, he reviewed the *actions* line again. He didn't want to sign it. Ray was a good cop. But the case had cost the department so much money. And ultimately, he'd failed in his assignment, despite catching the local distributor. There wasn't much he could do but recommend reinstatement once his mandatory leave was complete.

The phone rang, breaking his train of thought. Instinctively, Anderson grabbed the corded receiver and placed it to his ear. "Anderson!"

"James Anderson. How the hell are ya?" A grizzled voice echoed through.

There was no mistaking who it belonged to. "Kel'Gos, you ugly bastard, I wondered when you'd call. What can I do for you?"

"I may be ugly, but you're old. I'd wager my looks have held far better than yours!"

"That tends to happen when you're older than dirt itself."

"True. True. Listen, I was wanting to find out how Crum'Bul did down there in your neck of the woods. Do you think he's ready for a bit more responsibility?"

"To tell you the truth, Kelly. I believe he did just fine. He was a little naive when he first got here. But what rookie isn't? Hell, I'd go so far as to say he adjusted better than you did."

"Horseshit! I adjusted just fine. It was you that needed my help. Remember that, old man." Kel'Gos made certain to add emphasis to 'old'. "Things certainly have changed since we worked the field together."

"That they have. But much has stayed the same. Crum did a fine job. And if you want my input, I think he'll be okay wherever you place him." Anderson stated solemnly.

"That's what I wanted to hear. Anyway, enough of the pleasantries. With Pandora on the loose, I've convinced the Elders to let me build a new branch. I was thinking Miami is as good a place as any, if you'd be alright with that. I wouldn't want to step on your toes."

"I have no problem with it at all. The way things have gone this past week, it wouldn't surprise me if your kind is forced into the light in the near future. I'd be glad to have your men working with mine. Perhaps we can band together in unity to show the rest of the world that we aren't so different."

"As much as I'd love that, I think we need to take it a step at a time. Now, tell me about this human you had paired with Crum'Bul. My reports show they had a bit of a rough start. But they ended up getting on alright."

"I can agree with that. Ray Bradley is a good detective. And an even better cop. But he's impulsive, and at times a bit reckless. Overall, they worked well together. And he never told me about Crum'Bul. Which leads me to believe they were able to bond."

"Excellent! How would you feel about extending him an invitation to the WMD? I don't want to take a valuable asset from you, but I need a team to lead this new unit. And I was thinking of having your man and Crum'Bul run the show."

"To tell you the truth, Kelly. After this latest endeavor, I'm being forced to suspend him. If you think he'll work for your needs, make the offer. In the end, it's his choice."

"Sounds good. Hey, I've got to go. Someone just walked in. But when I'm down that way in the next month or two, keep a few days open. I want to do that fishing thing you showed me again."

"Will do. Goodbye, Kelly!"

The Pandora Gambit

Levi Samuel

Author's Notes

I hadn't planned to write this book as early as I did. But November happened. As those in the writing industry, or from my experience, anyone who is on social media, know, November is National Novel Writing Month, or NaNoWriMo. I won't go into the logistics of what it entails, but I will say that I typically avoid it.

This particular year, I wasn't given much choice. My friend George, whom I decided to dedicate this book to for his various encouragements and prompting in regard to advancing my career, called me up. He asked if I'd heard of NaNoWriMo. I explained I was aware of it, and why I never participate.

Needless to say, George being George, talked me into it. I was ready to write my other book, so I figured what the hell. I started writing. I got roughly 20k words into the story when I next spoke to George. He asked about my progress, and when I explained it was going well, he came back somewhat confused. It was at that point that I got an ear full.

He'd been under the impression I was going to write the story within these pages, as we'd talked about it quite a bit, but I wasn't ready. Long story short, I ended up jumping off my other book and starting this one with nothing more than a tailored concept. I hadn't done any research, no outline, no nothing. Over the course of thirty days (The length NaNo runs), I managed to do the aforementioned tasks, and completed my first draft of this book. I then went into edit mode, where I had to read it many times over, fix errors, and turn it into a cohesive story. But that wasn't the only obstacle I faced along the way.

Half way through this book, I saw a trailer for a movie called, Bright. Seeing the concept and how similar it was to my book, I became worried. I didn't want my story to be too similar to theirs. I was afraid people would accuse me of stealing the concept. But I couldn't go back and change everything I'd already done, so I kept working forward. And when the movie finally released, about the time I finished my first round of edits, I watched it. I was pleased to see they'd gone a different route than I had. If anything, their story could be 20+ years after this one, which I'm okay with.

I hope you've enjoyed this story as I've written it. If you'd like the latest updates on my new releases, as well as access to exclusive content, including a free book, feel free to join my newsletter at, http://eepurl.com/dxRUvL. I promise I won't spam you, and I only send out one or two emails a month.

Now it's time for me to return to my other projects. Thank you for reading, and please take a moment to leave a review with authorized online retailer. Whether you like the story or not, these reviews help us in ways you'll never know without becoming an author yourself. Thank you once again.

Levi Samuel
January 2018